Ten Ways to Make My Sister Disappear

NORMA FOX MAZER

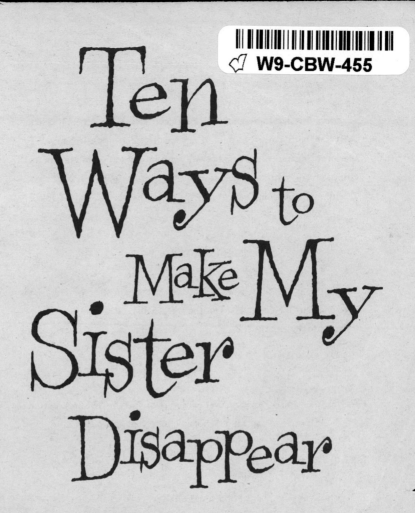

SCHOLASTIC INC.

New York Toronto London Auckland Sydney

Mexico City New Delhi Hong Kong Buenos Aires

ISBN-13: 978-0-545-05637-3

ISBN-10: 0-545-05637-3

Arthur A. Levine Books hardcover edition published by Arthur A. Levine Books, an imprint of Scholastic Inc., September 2007

12 11 10 9 8 7 6 5 4 3 2 1   8 9 10 11 12 13/0

Printed in the U.S.A.   40

First paperback printing, March 2008

Book design by Leyah Jensen

This one is for my

North Street neighbors.

What luck to have
landed in your midst!

And with thanks to

Marion Dane Bauer,

Anne Mazer,

and Ellen Miles,

each of whom read this
story at various stages and gave
me valuable comments.

Cont

ents

1

SPRIG EWING'S WORLD

TEN has always been Sprig's lucky number, and this is her tenth year, the best year ever. Being ten is *great*, so much better than nine. She absolutely feels older and more mature, and she's already looking forward to her next birthday, when she will be ten plus one or, as some people insist on calling it, eleven.

Sitting next to her older sister, Dakota, in the back of their car on the way to the airport on Sunday, January 10, Sprig checks her watch. 4:20 P.M. She was born on the tenth day of the tenth month at 4:10 P.M. At this very moment, she is exactly ten years plus three months plus ten minutes. "Mom!" She leans forward and taps her mother on the shoulder to give her this news.

Her mother glances into the rearview mirror. "What is it, sweetie?"

"Mom's driving. Stop distracting her," Dakota hisses into Sprig's ear. "Do you hear me? Answer, please."

"I hear you, I hear you," Sprig says. Dakota used to be so much nicer. It seems like a million years ago, but they used to play together, giggle about things, even sleep together, but when Dakota turned twelve in August? *Boom*, just like that, like something fell out of the sky and hit her on the head, she also turned bossy and know-it-all.

"Mom," Sprig says, "it's 4:20."

"I know," her mother answers. "It's a little late, but we'll get your father to the airport in time."

Her mother is not getting the significance of the moment. Anyway, now it's 4:21, the moment has passed, just like the whole day. Instead of lingering, as Sprig wanted it to, as so many days do, today has whirled by like the white, snowy world outside the car window. Just *whirled* by!

Maybe this is what Mom meant when Sprig

overheard her yesterday, saying to Dad, "Darn it, Larry, everything in life goes by too fast."

Too fast? No way! Aside from today, Sprig definitely does not agree with that. It takes *ages* for time to pass, especially when you're waiting for something, the way she's going to be waiting for Dad to return from his trip. She's already waiting for him to return, and he hasn't even left. The time ahead of her when he'll be away looms like doom. Like eternity. Like *forever.*

"Dads," she says, leaning forward. He's checking his e-ticket and doesn't answer.

"'Dads?'" Dakota says, behind her. "Excuse me, I don't think that's in the English language."

Sprig decides to maturely ignore her sister. She ruffles her father's hair and says, "Hello. I want to ask you something."

"Uh-huh. What is it, Baby?"

Grace is her real, proper name, it's right there on her birth certificate, but ever since Dad saw her for the first time (he was away when she was born) and called her "a little sprig of freshness," it's been either Sprig or Baby. He really should stop calling her that, even though she likes it when he does, maybe even *loves* it.

Dakota taps Sprig on the behind. "Hey. Now you're distracting Dad. He's got important things to think about. *Baby*," she adds.

"Oh, please, shut *up*," Sprig says.

"I'll take that whine with cheese."

"Funny."

"Thank you," Dakota says, flipping her hair behind her ears. "I thought so." Dakota has beautiful red hair, she's an A student, and last year in sixth grade, her classmates voted her Easiest to Get Along With. Last year, Sprig agreed. This year? *Not.*

"Today, of all days," Dakota goes on lecturing, "when Dad is going away, and the parents are stressed, you'd think you could control yourself."

"Quiet, you ugly beast." The words spring out of Sprig's mouth. She bites back a smile. She *loves* what she just said. It's not very often that she gets off a zinger that leaves her perfect sister speechless.

"Dads?" She leans farther over his seat until

her cheek rests against his. "Do you have to be gone for six whole weeks?" Maybe this time a miracle will occur, and the answer will be the one she wants. *Baby, I wouldn't stay away from my favorite daughter that long! I'll be back next week.*

She smooths his hair. He's so handsome — even if he is a little bit out of shape — and so smart that if he wanted to be President, he could just go for it. And how about his voice! It's great, really deep and, well, just *great*. He could be a pop singer. Or a songwriter. A long time ago, he made up this really funny song that he would sing to her. *I've got a little girl, she's kinda giggly, likes to twirl. Oh, yeah, yeah, yeah. I've got a little daughter, she's kinda skinny, could be fatter. Oh, yeah, yeah, yeah.* Of course, you have to say "datter," not daughter, to make it rhyme, but still, Sprig is sure he could be a great singer slash songwriter. Songwriters probably get to stay home most of the time.

Dad says he doesn't like traveling, but the thing is, he doesn't want to be anything but what he is, an architect slash engineer, a specialist in public buildings. About a dozen times a year, he's called away to consult with this company or that company, with this town or that city. Sometimes it's only for a day or two, but not this trip. He's going to Washington, D.C., to consult with some important government person — someone they call an undersecretary, which is a really weird title; it makes Sprig think of somebody crouching under a table. They're going to talk about building schools in Afghanistan. They might even decide to send Dad all the way over there. To where those awful people, the Taliban, went around shooting men who shaved and whipping women who tried to go to work. They wouldn't even let girls go to school!

"Dads," Sprig says again, "get your work done fast and come home sooner. Like in two weeks."

He's studying a bunch of papers spread out on his briefcase. "Hmm, maybe."

Sprig can tell he didn't really hear her. She speaks urgently to capture his attention. "Will you try? I don't see why a conference has to be so long. It seems stupid, Dad. And why —"

"Sprig, please," her mother says, peering out the window. "Can you keep it under wraps until — oh, darn! Larry, did I miss the turn? We're already running late."

"Easy, Lucie, it's the next one," her father says. He's always calm.

Dakota leans across the seat and prods Sprig in the arm. "See what you did with all your chatter? You made Mom almost miss the turn."

"You poked me!"

"Darling, I just touched you."

"Poked me!"

"I repeat," Dakota says, "I only touched you. And another thing, every time Dad goes away, you ask him the exact same questions."

"I don't, Dakota. I don't do that," Sprig says. Wondering if she does.

"The exact same questions," Dakota drones in her I-am-your-master voice. "You repeat yourself. Do you realize that's boring to people? Really *boring*."

"Mom," Sprig begins, but then, looking at her mother's hands clamped on the steering wheel and the way she's hunching her shoulders,

Sprig closes her mouth and stares out the window, thinking how great and wonderful and amazing and perfect and just plain *good* her life would be, if only two little — well, two big — things changed.

If only Dad didn't go away, *ever*.

And if only Dakota did, *forever*.

Say Dakota changes places with Dad. He stays home and she flies away. Say the plane flies to the Antarctic. Sprig can see it all: the plane landing, Dakota stepping out onto an ice floe, the beautiful white world, the amazing blue sky, and then . . . the wind . . . and Dakota floating gently, gently, oh so gently *away*. . . .

2

SMOOCHERINO FEVER

WHILE Dad waits in line to use the machine to get his boarding pass, Mom stays with him. They are holding hands.

"Mom's sad that Dad is going away," Dakota says.

"Me too," Sprig says. The girls are standing on the other side of the rope. "Me and Mom are sad."

"Mom and *I* are sad," Dakota says.

"You don't act sad, Dakota."

"I was correcting your grammar," Dakota says. "'Me and Mom' is illiterate."

"Oh, *excuse* me, Ms. English Teacher."

"And just because I don't make a big deal and cry boo-hoo-hoo, like some people, I won't mention names, doesn't mean I'm not sad about Dad. Anyway, I just wish he was staying home."

"I hate it when he goes away," Sprig says.

"Well, you can't do anything about it, so don't mope around. Are you going to say good-bye to him cheerfully?"

"Yesss."

"You're not going to cry?"

"Nooo."

"Promise?"

"Dakota. I said it! Leave me alone."

Sprig has already given herself a talking-to about crying — that is, about *not* crying — and she is resolved that not one tear is going to fall. And if she feels them coming, well, she has an emergency plan. She'll count to ten — silently, of course — and imagine each number as a different person. One, a skinny girl on a diet . . . two, a girl kneeling . . . three, a girl with sideways boobs . . . et cetera. By the time she gets to ten, skinny and her fat friend, she should be safely dry-eyed.

Good plan, she congratulates herself. She has always cried, as Mom says, at the drop of a hat. Mom used to hug her when it happened, but after her birthday two months ago, Mom and Sprig had a little talk. "Maybe, sweetie, you could work on not crying so much?" Mom said, and Sprig promised to try. End of talk.

She has been definitely trying, but it's hard not to cry when things happen, like failing your swimming test at the Y and, on the same day, your spelling test in school. And how can you not cry when you find a little yellow dog dead in the road, right across from your house? That afternoon, Sprig had run into the road and picked up the limp body, even though Dakota was yelling, "Stop, don't do that. Cars are coming! You're going to be roadkill!"

It was Dakota, though, who found the dog's name, Oscar, on his tags and who called the number and talked to the man who came to claim him. When the man saw Oscar lying stiff and cold on their steps, he picked up the dog and cradled him. "Oscar, my friend, I'm going to miss you." That's when Sprig started really crying.

Just remembering all this now, in the airport, makes her choke up.

"Hey," Dakota says. "Are you bawling already?"

"No." Sprig gulps and swipes her eyes with her sleeve.

"That's better," Dakota says. "Keep that crying thing under control. Mom and I know it's just your way of getting attention."

Sprig grabs her sister's arm. *That crying thing.* As if she turns it on and off, like a faucet. As if she does it for a reason. For *attention.* "Take that back!" she says.

"Pleeease," Dakota says with exaggerated courtesy. "You're being violent." She unpeels Sprig's fingers and straightens her jacket.

"Girls," Mom calls. Dad is finally done at the ticket machine, and he and Mom are walking toward the escalator.

Dakota grabs Sprig's hand, and they rush after their parents. As they jump onto the escalator, Dakota, who's wearing new boots with thick heels, stumbles and almost falls. Sprig latches onto her arm again and steadies her. "Saved you!" she says. "Are you grateful?"

"Tremendously. Thank you."

"You're welcome."

When they get to the security gate, their parents are waiting for them. Or are they? Do they even see that Dakota and Sprig are here? Mom and Dad have their arms around each other, and they're kissing. People are walking by them, and they don't even notice, they just keep kissing.

"Kill me now," Dakota says. "They're smooching like teenagers."

"Smoocherino fever!" Sprig says.

The sisters look at each other, and they can't help laughing.

3

GUESSING
GAMES

TUESDAY night, Mom and Dakota are making supper — a big salad with yummy blue cheese dressing, grilled salmon (which means delicious, crusty pieces of fish), pan-fried potatoes, and garlic bread. A perfect supper — Sprig's mouth waters, just thinking about it — but it would be more perfect if *she* was the one cooking with Mom. She can do everything Dakota can do, and mostly Mom lets them take turns, but sometimes, if she's in a rush, like tonight when she has knitting group, she gives Dakota extra turns.

Sprig finishes setting the table and Dakota pours dressing over the salad and puts it in the middle of the kitchen table. When Dad is home, they eat in the dining room. "Sit down, girls, fish is done, and I'll be right back," Mom says, running up the stairs. "I have to get my knitting stuff."

Dakota sits down and rearranges her silverware. "Fork on the left, knife and spoon on the right," she instructs.

"I like putting them all on one side," Sprig says. "Mom doesn't care."

"*I* care."

"Well, I don't," Sprig says.

"And I don't care that you don't care."

Does Dakota always have to have the last word? Sprig takes the salad tongs and claps them together, a nice crisp sound — the way her voice should be when she talks to her sister. "Dakota," she says. "Tonight when Dad calls, *I* talk to him first."

"Guess what! You're wrong."

"Nooo! Last night you talked to him first."

"That's right, because I'm older, and because you'll probably cry. Guess what, I'm giving you time to pull yourself together."

Sprig isn't sure which is more infuriating, Dakota's saying *guess what* or saying she'll cry.

True, she did cry last night when she talked to Dad, but only a little and only because she's not yet used to his being away. Every time he goes on one of his work trips, it's kind of like that. It's an *adjustment*.

Mom is back, and they sit down and start passing around the food. Almost immediately, the phone rings. Mom looks at the clock. "Too early for your father. He said he'd call around nine. Must be Marcy to tell me she's going to miss our knitting group."

"No, Mom, I'm sure it's Vicki Winters," Dakota says. "To borrow my math homework."

Guessing who's calling before anyone answers the phone is a family game. When Dad's home, he makes up really funny stuff, like the caller is a movie star, or someone to say he's won fifty-six million dollars in the lottery and does he have his ticket in a safe place?

Sprig wants to guess Dad, but Mom is probably right. As the phone rings again, and Mom stands to get it, Sprig says, "Um, Bliss Gardner." Her new best friend.

Mom winks at her, picks up the phone and says, "Hello?"

Sprig loves the way Mom says that, two notes and three syllables. Hel-low-oooh. Up the scale, then down. "Hel-low-oooh," she echoes after Mom.

"You're mimicking Mom?" Dakota says.

"No!"

"You're mocking her."

"I am not!"

"Don't try to wriggle out of it. I heard you."

"Girls," Mom says, smiling, "it's your dad."

Sprig pushes back her chair. So she was correct! She should have stuck to her guns. That's what Dad says — *Girls, stick to your guns.* Means, don't give up on what you know is right. Dad is so smart!

While she's thinking this, Dakota has taken the phone. Sprig makes fists and taps herself on the jaw. *Wake up!* she tells herself. Too late! Dakota is telling Dad *everything* — what they're having for supper, and how the school bus had to turn around this morning because the wind blew down a tree at the end of the street, and how, for a few minutes, they thought the school bus wouldn't be able to get through, and everybody was cheering.

Sprig was going to give Dad all that news! Now what does she have for him? *This morning, it was zero degrees. I saw the full moon last night. We have a substitute teacher. This is his second day. His name is Mr. Julius.* Ugh, so boring! Besides, she already told him about Mr. Julius.

Dakota's holding out the phone. It's her turn. "How are you, Baby?" Dad says.

"Good, Dads. How about you?"

"Terrific! I'm playing tennis every morning at the clubhouse in this building."

"Oh. That's good. Dads?"

"Yeah, sweetie?"

"I — I —"

"What is it?" He's laughing. "Don't make me guess."

"I miss you." Just three little words, but her throat clogs up.

"Hey, I've only been gone two days."

Sprig laughs with Dad, but it's a wobbly laugh, a *pathetic* laugh. So pathetic she could cry — and she does, but at least she's able to hold it off until she's in bed with the lights out and the blanket pulled over her head.

4

THE QUESTION THIEF

COMING off the school bus, Sprig stamps her feet, which are cold, cold, cold, even though she's wearing fur-lined boots. All up and down Baylor Street, the trees sparkle with their load of snow, and chimneys pour white smoke into the frosty air, smoke that rises into the sharp blue of the sky. She starts across the street, but Dakota grabs the back of her jacket.

"Whoa there!" Dakota says. "I didn't see you look both ways."

Sprig jerks free of her sister's grip. "Mr. Arnett has the STOP sign out. Look!" She points to the line of cars in front and in back of the bus.

"You still have to be careful."

"I know that! You tell me the same thing every day."

"I'm responsible for you when Mom is working, and guess what?" Dakota stays on Sprig's heels as they cross the street. "I don't want to be the one scraping you up off the pavement."

"Scraping me up off the pavement," Sprig mutters. "Nice!" She stamps up the driveway, crushing the icy ruts under her boots. *She* should be in charge of Dakota! Maybe she worries over a lot of things, but *she* is not boy-crazy. She does not and never will change her clothes a million times, as if she's going somewhere, and then end up in bed. *And*, if *she* had a younger sister, she would be much nicer to her. Which would be super-sensible, because then, guaranteed, her little — no, her *younger* — sister would love her to pieces.

As it is, Sprig has to lavish all her love on Miss Ruthie's Cora, who, right this minute, is stumbling down the driveway toward her. Sprig runs to meet her. "Cora, my sweetheart." She bends down to kiss her, and in return Cora kiss-licks Sprig's face all over with her soft tongue. Cora is nine, sixty-three in dog years. "I'm sorry you're so old," Sprig whispers into her ear. Cora still has four shining white paws to go with her brown coat, but she's also got arthritis in her joints and eyes dimmed by glaucoma.

"Hello, Sprig," Miss Ruthie calls down from her little square porch. "Hello, Dakota." Miss Ruthie has lived in the apartment over the Ewings' garage all of Sprig's life and, Sprig thinks, she's like a good old auntie with a little hearing problem and some funny habits. "Come up here, darling girls, and talk to me," she says. Leaning on the railing, her elbows plunked into the cake of snow, she's knitting, working away at her latest project.

"Sprig, leave Cora alone," Dakota says, giving her a push, "and go say hello to Miss Ruthie."

"You too." Sprig takes her sister's arm. "It's so cold out today, Dakota. Do you think Miss Ruthie's hands are warm enough?"

"Stop worrying about things that don't concern you," Dakota says, echoing Mom. "Miss Ruthie knows what she's doing. Don't forget, the older you get, the smarter you get. I'm older than you, and I'm way smarter."

"Yeah, right," Sprig says. "Ha-ha." She starts up the stairs, with Cora panting warmly behind her. "Miss Ruthie," she calls, pitching her voice high, "that scarf you're knitting is so pretty. The colors look like trees in the fall."

"You're adorable." Miss Ruthie beams at her. "So young and so smart."

"I'm not that young. I'm *ten*, remember?"

"Hello, Miss Ruthie," Dakota says, behind her. "That *is* a pretty scarf." And without missing a beat, she adds, "Are your hands warm enough?"

Sprig drops her backpack with a thump. That was her question! Dakota just flat-out stole it.

"Oh, I'm fine." Miss Ruthie puts down her knitting needles and holds out her hands to show that she's wearing half gloves. "But thank you for asking, dear. That's very thoughtful."

So! Not only did Dakota steal Sprig's question, she stole the praise for asking the question. It's a crime, a double crime! What would Judge

Judy say about *that*? She'd lean forward over her high desk and pound her gavel. *Dakota Ewing, you're a common question thief. I'm putting you away in the slammer.*

"Girls," Miss Ruthie is saying, "what do you hear from your father?"

"He's good, Miss Ruthie," Sprig says hastily. "He's playing tennis every morning at this clubhouse —"

"He's working hard," Dakota interrupts. "He has tons of meetings."

"He calls us every night," Sprig says.

"And she" — Dakota points to Sprig — "cries every time."

"Dakota!" Sprig glances at Miss Ruthie, then turns on her sister and says, low-voiced, "You shouldn't say that here. It's not . . . *loyal*."

Dakota shrugs, but her cheeks turn a bright red.

5

ORANGE CHALK AND A GIANT MOSQUITO

EXTENDING one of his long, spidery arms, Mr. Julius writes HOMEWORK on the blackboard in bright orange chalk. "Ugly color," Sprig says, under her breath. Her regular teacher, Mrs. Foote, always used either white or pale blue. Orange is *such* a bad choice but, anyway, what can you expect of a substitute, stand-in, not-the-real-thing teacher? Last week, Mrs. Foote had her baby. From the day Mr. Julius took over their class, it's been clear that he does *nothing* the way Mrs. Foote does. He talks too much, ends just about every sentence with "*okay?*," and his handwriting is weird, floppy, and loose, just like his arms.

"*Presenting My Family*," he scrawls on the

blackboard. More orange chalk. Maybe someone should tell him Halloween is long gone. "This is going to be a personal essay, kids. It will help me get to know you guys, okay? I'm going to give you plenty of time. Today's Thursday, okay? It won't be due until after the weekend, let's say on Tuesday. That's six days."

"Five," Russell Ezra-Evans calls out from behind Sprig.

"Good call." Mr. Julius throws the orange chalk up in the air and catches it. "No computers or printers, okay? Everything the old-fashioned way, so make sure I can read your handwriting. Any questions?"

Silence.

"No?" Mr. Julius sounds disappointed.

Sprig raises her hand. "Will you write a personal essay also?"

A few people in the room giggle, but Mr. Julius says, "That's an interesting idea, uh" — he looks down at his list of student names — "Grace."

"Sprig," she reminds him. "Remember? Everybody calls me Sprig."

"Oh, right. And, yes, Sprig, I'll write a personal essay."

"And will you read it out loud?"

"Don't mind her, Mr. Julius," Russell Ezra-Evans says from the seat behind Sprig, in his deep, man's voice. "She always asks questions." A moment later, Russell's foot makes contact with Sprig's leg. Maybe it's accidental. Yeah, right. He's always knocking into her. Thanks to their last names — Ewing and Ezra-Evans — ever since kindergarten Russell has been a pesky presence in Sprig's life.

"Actually, that's another excellent suggestion from Sprig —" Again, Mr. Julius looks down at his list of names.

"He's Russell Ezra-Evans." That's tiny Bliss Gardner, Sprig's friend, who sits across the aisle from her.

"Yes, I am," Russell booms to class laughter. "Last time I looked, that was me."

"He's so cute," Bliss says later, as they walk out of school together toward the parking lot.

The buses are lined up like yellow animals panting clouds of blue breath into the cold air.

"Who's cute?" Sprig asks.

"Russell."

"*Russell?*" Sprig says. "Please tell me you didn't say that."

"No, I mean it. Really, he's sort of adorable."

"About as adorable as a giant mosquito."

"Come on, think about it. The way he's always teasing on you? You can tell he doesn't mean anything bad by it. He likes you."

"Russell does not like me. He hates me."

They stop by Sprig's bus, number 380. It's carrying a layer of wind-blown snow on the roof. "He probably wants to be your boyfriend," Bliss says.

"Ewww, no! If I wanted a boyfriend, it would not be Mr. Supersize, Mr. Giant Mosquito, Mr. Huge, Mr. Humongous, Mr. —"

"Stop," Bliss says, but she's laughing. "That's so mean. Don't you feel the least bit sorry for him? It must be hard to be so much bigger than everyone else."

"I have no pity for that bozo."

"Well . . ." Bliss shifts her backpack. "Maybe you should. I know what that feels like, being different from everyone."

"You do not," Sprig says.

"I do! I'm always the shortest one, the smallest one, and you know what? There's always someone who's gonna pat me on the head, like I'm a baby or a dog or something."

Sprig can't resist. She pats Bliss on the head. "You mean, like this?"

"Hey!" Bliss pushes her hand away. "Don't do that!"

"Sor-ry." Sprig back-steps. "You really don't like that, do you?"

"I *seriously* don't like it." Bliss's face is scrunched up tight. "It makes me really —" She takes in a breath. "Oh, forget it." She looks past Sprig toward the other side of the parking lot. "There's my bus, I have to go."

"Wait a second," Sprig says. "Are you mad at me?"

"No," Bliss says, sounding like *yes*. "Bye. See ya." She walks off, her hands supporting the weight of her backpack.

"Bliss? Bliss!" Sprig runs after her. "I didn't mean to hurt your feelings or anything. I wouldn't want to hurt you!"

Bliss looks at her for a moment as if she's deciding something, then she says, "I know that."

"So is it okay?" Sprig says and, without waiting for an answer, she throws her arms around Bliss. They hug for a moment. One of the bus drivers is sitting on his horn.

"Gotta go," Bliss says, and she runs for the bus.

"What was that all about?" Dakota strolls up, arm in arm with Krystee Hampler, her best friend this year, a tall girl with a sarcastic tongue and bright green eyes, which she can cross at will.

Krystee tugs on Sprig's ponytail. "Little girls having a fighty-fight and kissy making up?"

"None of your business," Sprig says. "Get your hands off my hair."

"What a charming child," Krystee croons and crosses her eyes at Sprig. With a little effort, Sprig manages to cross her eyes back at Krystee. "Dakota," Krystee shrieks gleefully, "your little baby sister is funny. *Not!*"

All the way home, on the smelly, overheated bus, that phrase, *little baby sister*, repeats itself in Sprig's mind. Three words that taken separately are, well, *okay*, but put together? Totally annoying!

6

THE CUTEST BOY
ON THE MOON

"**SPRIG**," Mom calls from her bedroom. "Come here, please."

"I'm almost ready, Mom," Sprig yells. She yanks at her blue shirt, clattering the hanger to the floor.

"Oh, please, make some more noise," Dakota says. She's at her desk. "I'm only trying to study here."

Sprig pulls on the shirt and sticks her feet into her clogs. Tonight is the monthly Mother-Daughter Reading Club meeting at the library, a special thing she and Mom do together. "These buttons are wicked tiny," she says, fumbling with the last two.

"C'mere," Dakota beckons without looking up. Sprig goes over to her, and Dakota finishes the buttoning. "There you are." She pats Sprig on the cheek, a little too hard. "Now *go*, will you?"

Sprig picks up her book, a fantasy called *Water Shaper* about this princess named Margot. She has ten more pages to read, but she's been putting it off, not wanting the story to end. That's what she'll say in Reading Club tonight. *When I read a really good book like this one, it's as if I'm not even here anymore. I'm in the story. Everything disappears, like my house, my room, my sister . . .* she *totally disappears, and that's just* great*!* Well, maybe not that last part about Dakota, not with Mom right there.

She clops across the hall. Mom's lying on the bed, her hand over her eyes, the afghan Miss Ruthie made for her pulled up over her shoulders. "Mom," Sprig says. "Are you sleeping? I'm ready."

Mom half sits up. "I have a terrible headache. It's been coming on all day, but it just hit me." She falls back against the pillow. "I'm sorry, honey," she says, covering her eyes again. "I don't think I can make it tonight."

For a moment, Sprig is so disappointed she

can hardly speak. "Do you want me to bring you anything?" she asks finally. "Like tea or something?"

"No. I just need . . . sleep. . . ." Mom murmurs. "Thanks, sweetie."

Sprig tiptoes out and closes the door. "Mom has a headache," she tells Dakota. "We're not going to the Reading Club."

"Crap," Dakota says. "I wanted some privacy. What are you going to do now?"

"Work on my essay, I guess. I have to hand it in tomorrow, and I'm only half done."

"When did you think you were going to finish it?"

"Tomorrow morning."

Dakota shakes her head. "Great planning. You better go do it."

"Can I have the desk?"

"No, you can't have the desk. Go work on the dining room table. Go on. *Go.*"

Sprig sits down on her bed and crosses her arms. "If I want to stay here, you can't kick me out."

Dakota spins around on her chair. "I know, I know, I *know*! Do you think the parents will ever buy a house with another bedroom, so I can have my own room?"

"Mom says it's hard to find the time to look when they're both working, and Dad's away and everything." Sprig falls silent, thinking of Afghanistan. After a while, she gets up. "Okay, I'm going to work in the dining room. You can have your privacy. I bet you're going to IM your beloved Krystee."

"I might," Dakota says. She already has the computer turned on.

Later, Sprig is nearly finished with her essay when Dakota appears and flings herself into a chair. "Sprig. What do you think about boys?"

Is this a trick question? "Boys? They're okay. They're, you know, *boys*."

"I love them," Dakota says. "Guess who Krystee and I think is the cutest boy in the whole school!" Dakota's cheeks are very pink. "He's probably the cutest boy in the whole United States. If we lived on the moon? He would be the cutest boy on the moon, no contest. So can you guess? It's someone you know."

Sprig pushes her paper aside. Talking to Dakota like this is much more fun than writing an essay. "I know a ton of boys. Give me a clue."

"It's someone you see every day."

The name that pops into Sprig's head is Russell Ezra-Evans. Which is ridiculous. Cutest boy? Not even in the running.

"Give up?" Dakota asks. "Okay, it's Thomas. Buckthorn." Thomas Buckthorn is in Dakota's class. He has dark curly hair and long eyelashes, and a group of noisy boys are always around him on the school bus.

"I know Thomas," Sprig says.

"Of course you do. Duh." Dakota springs up. "So is he the cutest or —" She stops, looking over Sprig's shoulder. "What are you writing there?" She snatches up the paper and reads aloud, "'My sister, Dakota, is obsessed with her hair. She combs it for at least an hour every morning.' That is crap! And who gave you permission to write *anything* about me? Cross that out right now."

"Dakota, I can't mess it up with cross-outs." Sprig smooths out her paper. "I told you, I have to hand it in tomorrow."

"No way you're going to hand in that I comb my hair for an hour every morning. That is an utter, total *lie*."

"You comb it for a long time."

"Not an hour."

"How long? I mean, exactly how long?"

"Ten minutes, tops."

"I'm sure it's more. I'll time you tomorrow morning."

"Not unless I give you permission. And I do not. And I do not give you permission to write about me." Dakota's hands come down on Sprig's shoulders. *"No permission."*

"Stop breathing on my neck. And get your creepy hands off me."

"Will do," Dakota says, and reaches for Sprig's paper.

"No!" Sprig yells. For a moment, they're both tugging on the paper. The inevitable happens — it rips.

"Sorry, Sprig," Dakota says, letting go.

"Now I have to start all over," Sprig wails.

"Well..." Dakota pats her shoulder. "Think of it this way. When you rewrite, you'll do an even better essay. Especially leaving my hair out of it," she adds.

Sprig stares at the torn, wrinkled mess in front of her. If only Dakota were a piece of paper! She'd crumple her up. Litter the floor with her. And sweep her into the wastebasket, before Mom even noticed that her darling daughter was gone.

Sprig Ewing

Personal Essay for Mr. Julius' class

My Family

Hello! I am Grace Blue Ewing, but I am called Sprig by everyone. I espechally like my middle name, since blue is and always will be my favorite color. My family is me, my sister and my parents, and they are mostly great, but when I think about it, I realize everyone has a problem.

My father's problem is that he really doesn't like to be away from us, but he loves his job, and he has

to travel for it. He's an engeneer
and architect, and right now, he's in
Washington, D.C., consulting with the
government. When he's home he
can be litehearted and a lot of fun.

My mother is a more sereous
person, except when we all go on
vacation together [last year we went
to Gettysburg], and then she can get
silly and be a lot of fun. She's a
bank manager, which is a responsible
job, so her problem is she never has
enough time for everything.

My sister's problem is that she
thinks she has no problems. She
thinks because she's older that she's

superor to me, which is extremly
annoying. She is always correcting me
and saying she knows what I should
do and that she is smarter because
she's older. Which I think is basically
ridiculus.

Can you tell that my problem
is basically my sister? I'm usually a
happy person, except when she's
bothering me. I love to read, it's almost
my hobby. I also love to ski in winter,
swim in summer, daydream and make
lists. I love animals, but my mother is
highly allergic, so we can't have any
pets, but our friend Miss Ruthie has
Cora, who's a very lovable dog. Miss

Ruthie is like an honorary member of our family. We all love her. I don't think she has any problems, except that she's getting old, which is Cora's problem, too, besides being half blind. I worry about Cora. Sometimes I worry that I worry too much.

I hope I have given you a good picture of my life and my family.

THE END

7

RISING, RISING, RISING

"**SPRIG!** Dakota!" Miss Ruthie is standing on her porch, waving to them, as they come up the driveway after school. "I have something to ask you," she sings out. She's wearing her long puffy green coat with a cap pulled down over her ears.

"What's that, Miss Ruthie?" Sprig runs up the steps and hugs Cora, who's grinning at her.

"I'm going to Boston next Saturday to visit my brother and my nieces. I'll go on the bus early Saturday morning and be back Sunday night, and I need someone to look after Cora. Feed her, walk her, make sure she does her business, all that. Would one of you like the job?"

"Yes," Sprig and Dakota say, at the same moment, but of course Dakota says it louder, and of course she has the sense to add, "I would be really happy to do it, Miss Ruthie."

"Wonderful. Both of you are just wonderful. Tell me, what do you think would be fair pay? Remember, it's two whole days."

Why be paid at all? Sprig thinks. Taking care of Cora would be fun, not work. Besides, Miss Ruthie doesn't have a lot of money. Sometimes she takes care of children, and sometimes she fills in for her friend Nadine, who works at The Fashion Shoppe, but she doesn't have a regular job.

"Miss Ruthie?" Dakota says. "You can pay me whatever you think is fair."

"Me too," Sprig says hastily. "That's what I was going to say."

"That's very sweet," Miss Ruthie says to Sprig. "But you know what, dear, we'll let Dakota do it this time. Come in the apartment with me, Dakota. I'll show you where everything is, the food and Cora's treats and her toys and her bed."

Dakota brushes past Sprig and follows Miss Ruthie inside. Sprig buries her face in Cora's warm, stinky fur. "*I* know where your food is," she tells Cora. "And your bed, and your toys. I know how much to give you to eat, one third of a can two times a day, and one scoop of dry. I would take good care of you, Cora, better than Dakota! I'd throw the ball for you, and be patient, and not rush you doing your business."

Will Dakota do all that? Maybe . . . and maybe not. But Dakota got the job. She always gets all the good stuff, stays up the latest, sees the most TV shows, and talks to Dad first and longest. It's just not fair.

"You know what I wish, don't you, Cora?" The dog licks Sprig's face and gazes sympathetically at her. "Not that I would want anything *bad* to happen to Dakota," Sprig adds. No, despite everything, she just wants her to go, the way smoke goes in winter. In all the cold weeks, you see the white smoke curling out of the chimneys, sometimes going straight up into the air, sometimes taken this way and that by the wind, but always, *poooof,* it disappears. It's gone. If smoke can do it, why not a person? Why not Dakota?

Leaning her head against Cora's warm back, Sprig narrows her eyes and looks up into the sky, and, *yes*, she sees her sister up there. Dakota in a gauzy, smoky white dress that floats around her like, well, smoke. And like smoke rising, Dakota too is rising. Rising, rising, rising. Becoming smaller and smaller, fainter and fainter . . . until . . . *poooof* . . . she's gone.

8

TOMATOES AND CUCUMBERS

"**W**HAT are you trying to do, Sprig, kill that hamburger?" Standing at the sink, Dakota shakes the lettuce in the colander. "Hurry up, I want to get everything done before Mom comes home."

"I'm almost finished." Sprig takes another chunk of hamburger and slaps the meat between her palms. She loves this job, the rhythmic *slap slap slap*. It reminds her of being little and playing with clay, and how she used to think about things when she did that.

She's thinking about things now too, thinking about how Dakota got that job away from her *slap slap slap* and how today is the tenth day *slap slap slap slap slap slap* that Dad has been gone. Okay, she has to think about something else, like the Mighty Pest and how Bliss keeps saying he's cute, and how maybe Mr. Julius will think her essay is just wonderful and give her an A and —

"Okay, stop!" Dakota has come over and is inspecting the plate of raw patties. "That's plenty. Wash your hands and get me the tomatoes."

"Get them yourself. I'm not your servant, Dakota," Sprig says, but she ambles over to the refrigerator, takes a tomato from the vegetable bin, and puts it on the far end of the counter so Dakota has to reach for it.

"Just one?" Dakota says. "Mom likes a lot of tomatoes in the salad. Get me some more. They're a very important fruit."

"Ha, ha, you mean vegetable."

"Ha, ha, I mean *fruit*. Tomatoes are fruit, for your information, and they're way good for you. Tons of vitamin C, vitamins A and K, plus potassium, plus —"

"Okay, okay. Don't give me a food lecture." Sprig flings open the refrigerator door.

"While you're there," Dakota says, "get me a couple of cucumbers too."

"Say please."

"Come on, Sprig, just get me the stuff."

Sprig's hand hovers over the vegetable bin. "Okay, now you have to say, 'Please get me tomatoes and cucumbers, my beloved Sprig.'"

"In your dreams, girl. Just get me the stuff." When Sprig doesn't move, Dakota sighs and says, *"Please."*

Later, as they're finishing supper, Dad calls. Mom talks to him first. Before she takes the phone into the dining room for privacy, she says, "Girls, you did a great job on supper. I'll tell your father."

"Let's surprise Mom and clean up too," Dakota says, and starts clearing the table. "I'll do the dishwasher, you sweep. I talk to Dad next," she adds.

"No," Sprig says. "I want to talk to him next."

"Sorry, tonight it's in order of age. Mom, then me, then you."

Dakota's logic is perfect — and maddening. Sprig grabs the broom and sweeps furiously around her sister.

Dakota jumps out of the way, her white shirt

billowing out over her green pants. Green and white, same colors as the cucumbers she cut into their salad. Is it possible that Dakota is a cucumber in disguise? Sprig rolls this idea around in her mind. With just a touch of imagination, she can see it. Yes, she can definitely see Dakota as a cucumber, one of those juicy, crunchy cucumbers. A cucumber fit for the salad bowl. *Crunch, crunch.* Yum, yum. Down the hatch. Bye, bye, cucumber. Bye, bye, Dakota.

Crunching up Dakota puts Sprig in a good mood again, and when it's her turn to talk to Dad, she greets him exuberantly. "Dads! Here I am. Last, but not least!"

He laughs, and says, "You are so right, my baby." Which makes her feel even better, and they have a really good conversation. Just before they hang up, he asks her if she knows anything about Afghanistan.

"A little," Sprig says. "Didn't they have those people called the Taliban, who were so bad they wouldn't even let girls go to school? And, uh, they had a lot of war there, but it's over now. I think it is," she adds.

"Good beginning," Dad says approvingly. "That's my girl. Look up Afghanistan in the atlas," he goes on. "The one I keep on my desk in Mom's and my study. Read about the country, or you can go on the Net. Check out their food, architecture, things like that."

"Why do you want me to do that, Dad?"

"It's one of my interests," he says. "A fascinating place — the art, the people — great people. We'll talk about it again."

9

BAD
NEWS

GOING home on the school bus, Sprig is trying to remember everything she ever read or heard or saw on the news about Afghanistan, so she can tell Dad when he calls. Last year, Miss Ruthie made that afghan for Mom's birthday, squares of purple and violet and green. Mom keeps it on the foot of her bed. Do they make afghans in Afghanistan? It sounds like a riddle. She'll have to look that up too, and tell Dad.

The bus lumbers slowly through the snow-clogged streets. In the seat behind her, Dakota and Krystee are whispering about boys. Doesn't Dakota care about anything else? She probably never even talks to Krystee about Dad and

Afghanistan. "He's a ten," she hears Dakota saying.

"I'd only give him an eight," Krystee says. "Or maybe a seven and a half."

"You're crazy, Buckthorn is at least a nine."

Sprig twists around. "Will you two please shut up? I'm trying to think here."

"The child is trying to think," Krystee says. "I am *so* impressed."

Next Krystee will cross her eyes. Why doesn't she try that lovely trick on Thomas Buckthorn? The cutest boy on the moon is sitting on the back bench in the middle of a tangle of his friends, who are taking turns giving each other shots in the arm.

"We are having a private conversation," Dakota says. "Turn around, please."

"Turn, doggy," Krystee says.

"Arf. Arf," Dakota chimes in, elbowing Krystee.

How mean. It's Krystee's fault! She's a total bad influence on Dakota. To Sprig's dismay, her eyes fill. She doesn't *really* care that they're being mean, and she's sure she wouldn't care at all, if Dad was home.

"Doggy," Dakota says, sounding just like the Bad Influence. "Are you going to cry?"

Is she going to cry? In front of *them*? No! Sprig blinks hard, blinks furiously to hold back the tears. She blinks and blinks and blinks, until Dakota blurs in front of her wet eyes and disappears in a puddle of shimmery dots.

That night, waiting for Dad to call, and already in her pj's, Sprig is looking out the bedroom window at the snowy field behind their house. The waxing moon is almost full, and the field is so bright that she gets caught up in a dream of dancing across that icy slickness, her feet never touching the snow, never feeling the cold. Oh, how graceful she is! All up and down Baylor Street people pour out of their houses to watch her and take her picture. She dances away from the window, dances around the room, between the beds, raising her arms, bending and dipping and —

"What are you *doing*?" Dakota says.

Sprig stops abruptly. Great. Now Dakota will

channel Krystee and say something mean like *the whole house is shaking*, or *first time I ever saw a dog dance*. Instead, Dakota grabs Sprig's hands and dances around the room with her. "Faster, faster," Dakota orders, and they whirl and stamp and gallop together until they collapse on Dakota's bed, laughing and out of breath.

The next morning, Sprig and Dakota are making their lunches at the table when Mom puts down her coffee cup and says, "Girls, last night you were sleeping when your father called. It was almost one o'clock. I was sound asleep myself!"

"Why'd he call so late?" Sprig says.

"I was going to stay up," Dakota says, "but I got too tired."

"He was in a meeting that ran really, really late," Mom says. "Some important decisions were being made, and that's what I need to talk to you both about."

Sprig freezes, holding the mustard knife in mid-air. She doesn't like the sound of that word *need*. Or the one that came before — *decisions*.

"Your father's going to be in a lot of meetings

in the next few days." Mom glances at her watch.

"What kind of meetings?" Dakota asks.

"We'll talk about all this in more detail later, but the long and the short of it is that, fairly soon, your father will be going —"

"Mom," Sprig interrupts. A blob of mustard falls to the table. "Mom, we need bread and —"

"Sprig, let me finish what I'm saying, please."

Maybe Sprig doesn't want Mom to finish. Maybe her somersaulting stomach doesn't want to hear what Mom is about to say. "Lettuce too. I can go to the store after school if you —"

"*Sprig.*" Mom takes her arm. "Listen to me, honey. You need to hear this. Your dad will be going to Afghanistan soon."

"Afghanistan," Sprig repeats. So it is bad news.

"We're not sure of the date yet," Mom says, "but he'll probably be leaving within the next week or so. He'll want to talk to both of you about it, of course, and —"

"Why is he going there?" Sprig says. "Afghanistan is so far away!"

"Well, yes," Mom says. "But he'll be doing what he always does, consulting about buildings, in this case, schools. That's a really good thing, and he's excited to be part of this project."

"Mom, what if something happens to him?" Sprig's voice comes out small.

"Nothing's going to happen to Dad," Dakota snaps. "Don't be stupid."

Sprig crushes her sandwich into a baggie. Mustard is smeared all over. "People are getting hurt over there. Even killed. Like Iraq! I saw it on the news."

"Your father's going to Kabul, that's the capital. The U.N. is there to protect people. He won't be going into the danger area." Mom glances at her watch again. "Look, we'll talk about this a lot more, but right now I have to get going, and you girls hustle too, or you'll miss your bus." She kisses Sprig on the head. "Try not to worry, honey."

Sprig nods. She listens as Mom leaves the house. She listens to the sound of the car crunching down the driveway. "Come *on*," Dakota says. "Why are you just standing there?" She stuffs

Sprig's lunch into her backpack and hands it to her. "Hey," she says, "get that zombie look off your face."

Sprig puts on her coat and boots and follows Dakota out of the house. Miss Ruthie is at her window, waving to them. "Hi, Miss Ruthie," Sprig says in a little voice.

"Why are you talking like that?" Dakota looks up. "Hi, Miss Ruthie!" she yells.

"Dakota —" Still, the little voice. "I don't want Dad to go there."

"Well, do you think I do?"

"No."

"You've got that right, anyway. Besides, he isn't going this minute. Maybe something will happen, and the plans will change."

"Really? Do you really think that could happen, Dakota?"

Dakota leans out over the curb, looking for the bus. "I said it, didn't I?"

10

CHIMPS

"**I STILL** think taking care of Cora should have been my job," Sprig says. She and Bliss are sprawled on Sprig's bed, with a plate of chocolate chip cookies between them. It's Friday afternoon. Tomorrow morning Miss Ruthie is going to Boston.

"Totally right," Bliss says loyally. She's sleeping over. So is Krystee. Ugh. "Like, guess who's the animal lover." Bliss points to the pictures of boy singers on Dakota's side of the room, and then to Sprig's wall with its pictures of chimpanzees and dogs. She takes another cookie, munches, and makes appreciative sounds. "These are so good! You could be a professional baker."

"No thanks. I want to do animal research, like Jane Goodall. Right in the jungle with the chimpanzees. I mean, if there are any left. They're an endangered species, and they're our closest relatives. Bliss, we're letting members of our own family die!"

"Cousins I never knew I had." Bliss scratches under her arms, hunching her shoulders and making huffing chimp noises.

"Bliss, do you know how intelligent they are? They use tools, they're problem-solvers, they don't talk like we do, but they communicate, and they have fabulous memories. We share ninety-eight percent of our genes with chimps."

"That's awesome," Bliss says. "I have to tell that to my dad. He loves numbers — it's the math-teacher thing. Did I tell you that he wants me to be a math teacher? He thinks it's the greatest job."

"You're good in math too. Do you want to do that?"

Bliss shakes her head. "I'm more the social-worker type, like my mom."

"I'm definitely going to do something different from my parents." Sprig rolls over and stares up at the stars painted on the ceiling. Mom put them up there, ages ago. "My mom is always working late and thinking about problems. My dad, you know what my dad does, I told you about him and Afghanistan." As soon as she says that, she has to clear her throat.

Just then, Dakota walks in with Krystee. "Time's up," Dakota says. "Good-bye. This is our room. We need our privacy."

"Why don't you two sleep in the parents' study?" Sprig says.

Dakota smooths her beautiful red hair behind her ears. "You guys are sleeping there. We agreed, that's the plan."

"That's what I heard," Krystee drawls. "Don't be a brat." As if it's her house.

Sprig picks up the plate of cookies. "Come on, Bliss. Let's go!"

Bliss follows her to the door, but then she stops and says sweetly, "Krystee. Do you know that you're a first cousin to a chimpanzee?"

"*What?*" Krystee says.

Sprig and Bliss are still laughing when they close the door to the study. "That was so perfect," Sprig says. "It was brilliant."

"Well, you told me," Bliss says modestly.

They set to work, first blowing up the camp mattresses, then unrolling the sleeping bags. "This is so fun," Bliss says. "Like camping, without the bugs. That girl Krystee — why is your sister friends with her?"

"I don't know. Fatal attraction or something." Sprig lies down to test the mattress. "You know what, Bliss, sometimes I love my sister, and sometimes I just *hate* her. Do you think that's sick and terrible?"

"Sometimes I hate my little brother."

Sprig sits up. "No way! I thought everything was perfect in your family."

"I wish. My parents dote on Spence, he can't do anything wrong, and whatever happens, it's, like, always my fault." She smooths out the sleeping bag. "Let's talk about something else. Something silly. What's your favorite color?"

"Blue . . . of course — my middle name. And ten is my favorite number. I like to make lists of ten things — like my ten favorite foods or my ten best ideas. Or ten ways to make my sister disappear. I thought of a good one yesterday when I was baking the cookies. If I could mix Dakota into the dough and bake her —"

"Then eat it?" Bliss can't stop laughing. "Now that is sick. Do you really have ten things like that?"

"I'm still working on it. Want to see?" Sprig roots around in her backpack, then pulls out her list and hands it to Bliss.

"I just thought of one for you," Bliss says after she reads the list. She grabs her knees and rocks excitedly. "Put your sister on a raft and float her out to the ocean!"

"That's good. I'm going to write it down."

"Here's another one I just made up. Send her around the world in a hot-air balloon! Do you like that one?"

"I love it," Sprig says, scribbling.

"It's really not original," Bliss says apologetically. "We all watched *Around the World In Eighty Days* last weekend."

"Sprig," Mom says, coming in. "How are you doing, honey?" Mom's in her working clothes, a dark skirt and a gray pleated blouse. "Bliss, *hello*," she says, in that way Sprig loves. She bends over and kisses Sprig. "I see you two are all settled. The beds are okay?"

"Totally! They're supercomfy," Bliss says enthusiastically, the way she says almost everything, the way she said, *Put her on a raft and float her out to the ocean!*

For Bliss, Sprig realizes, her ten ways list is just another game, and in a way it is for Sprig too — but it's also more. Every time she thinks of a new way, it's like letting out a breath that she's been holding.

And now, with Bliss's two great ideas, she has nine ways of making Dakota disappear. Too bad she didn't think of them herself. "Do you think it's sort of cheating to take your ideas?" she asks Bliss, after Mom leaves.

"No," Bliss says. "Everyone has different ideas. That's how inventions and discoveries happen. My mom says that being open to new ideas makes your life juicy."

"*Juicy,*" Sprig repeats. "Cute! That gives me another idea." She smooths out the paper and writes, then shows it to Bliss.

"Euuuw," Bliss says. "Poor Dakota!"

Ten Ways
to Make My Sister Disappear

1. Dakota steps onto an ice floe in the Antarctic... and drifts off.
2. Put her in prison for stealing my question.
3. A cucumber she is... and I crunch her...
4. If she were made of paper... oh, so many choices! Crumple! Rumple! Tear and toss!
5. Like smoke, she rises into the air, and, poooof.....
6. I blink her into a watery puddle.
7. Bake her like a cookie...

8. Float her out to the ocean on a raft.

9. Put her in a hot air balloon and send it around the world.

10. Juice her like an orange and drink her down.

11

THE APPEARANCE OF THOMAS BUCKTHORN

SATURDAY morning, Krystee's mother comes for her right after they finish breakfast, so she can go to her flute lesson. Fifteen minutes later, Bliss's father picks her up to take her to gymnastics class. And at nine o'clock, Mom drives Miss Ruthie to the bus station, and Dakota takes Cora for a walk.

Sprig is shoveling a path to Miss Ruthie's steps. It's one of those cold, blue winter days. A squirrel tunnels through the snow, disappears, then pops up, cheeks pouched and face splatted with white. "I see you're gathering nuts," Sprig says.

"No way," someone says behind her. It's Thomas Buckthorn on cross-country skis, a pole in each hand, a red ski cap pushed to the back of his curly black hair.

"Where'd you come from?" she says.

Thomas points to the wooded hill behind their house. "I live over there, on the other side of Poke Hill. So, what're you doing?"

"Hello?" She holds up the shovel, then scrapes up a shovelful and tosses it to the side. "See Sprig. See Sprig shovel snow."

Thomas is not amused. No sense of humor. Or maybe it wasn't funny? Maybe she was channeling sarcastic Krystee — *bad* thought. She rests her chin on the handle of the snow shovel and looks Thomas over. Maybe no sense of humor, but Dakota is right — definitely cute.

He slides back and forth on his skis. "You getting paid for doing that?"

"No."

"Then why are you doing it?"

"This is part of the stuff I do for my allowance."

"I get paid for everything I do," he says. "My father is a businessman, and he says getting paid for what you do is the way to learn the value of money."

"Do you get paid for breathing, and eating, and sleeping?"

"That's really funny," Thomas says. "I guess I should laugh."

"Oh, don't bother," Sprig says.

"Okay, I won't."

For a few moments, the only sounds are the scrape of the shovel and the slippery *swiiish* of Thomas's skis, as he poles back and forth. Why is he hanging around? "Do you want something?" Sprig finally says.

"Just wondering if you ski." She nods. "Downhill or cross-country?"

"Both."

"So . . . what about your sister? Does she like to ski?"

Okay, Sprig gets it now. "Yes, she does."

"Cross-country or —"

"Both. Like me."

Thomas shushes back and forth on his skis. "So . . . where is she?"

"Working."

"Oh. She's getting paid?" Sprig guesses that this is points in Dakota's favor. "Like, what does she do?"

He keeps saying *she.* "Buckthorn," Sprig says. "My sister has a name."

He gives her a smile. "So, *Sprig,* where is *Dakota?*"

She points downtown, toward the park. "Walking our neighbor's dog."

He gives her another dazzling smile and pushes off.

Sprig watches as he skis smoothly across the field, arms and legs working in a steady rhythm. He is definitely cute. He was nice enough too. *And* he knew her name. "Hey, Thomas!" she calls. "Thomas Buckthorn!"

She's not sure why she calls him. She packs a snowball and turning to the side (the way Dad taught her), she throws it as hard as she can at Thomas's retreating back. By then, though, he's so far into the field that the snowball never even gets close.

12

AIR
KISSES

SUNDAY morning, Dad calls early. "Baby," he says, when he talks to Sprig. "Mom tells me you're upset about my going to Afghanistan."

"Oh, no," she says, wanting to sound brave.

"This trip is a chance for me to do some real good," he says, "something that counts."

"You're always doing good things, Dad."

"This is a special opportunity. Listen, once there were six thousand schools in Afghanistan and probably not enough, even so, but most of the schools have been destroyed in the last couple decades."

"I googled Afghanistan the other night, Dad. It's not safe there. I want you to be safe."

"Sprig. Girls couldn't go to school under the Taliban. They had to stay in the house, and their mothers couldn't work. Think about it, honey. The only things women and girls were allowed to do were cook, clean, and take care of the children."

"That's so stupid," Sprig says.

"Right! And that's exactly why you can be glad that I'm going to be involved in planning schools. Schools for girls. Schools that won't exclude girls."

"But what if they do?"

"No, that's not going to happen, or I won't have anything to do with this project. That's a promise from me to you. I want you to be proud of your father."

"I *am*," she says. "I am proud of you."

"Okay, then we're on the same page about this trip, aren't we? Will you give me that, honey?"

"Okay, Dad," she says, loving the approval in his voice. "Same page."

But later, scooping up the last soggy cornflakes from her bowl, she wonders how she came to agree that it's a good thing he's going to Afghanistan. She didn't mean to say that!

"Sprig?" Dakota comes galloping into the kitchen, her ski boots laced over her shoulder. "Sprig, you have to help me. I totally forgot that Krystee and I were going skiing this morning and —"

"Where're you going?" Sprig says. "Can I go?"

"No you can't go! Sorry," she adds, not sounding sorry at all. "Krystee's mom is picking me up in five minutes." Dakota's voice rises. "And I have to take Cora out for her walk and feed her."

Sprig waits a beat, and then says, "I'll feed Cora and take her for a walk."

"You will! Oh, good sister!" Dakota hands her the key to Miss Ruthie's apartment. "Don't forget to wash Cora's dish," she says. "And rinse out the dog food can and put it in the recycle bin under the sink."

"I know, I know." Sprig tosses the key into the air and catches it, the way Mr. Julius catches the orange chalk.

Dakota pours a glass of milk and gulps it down. "There! Tell Mom I had breakfast. Oh, and would you sort of clean up Miss Ruthie's kitchen, like sweep the floor and wipe the counters? We don't want her to come back to a mess."

"Dakota, you're supposed to do all that. It's part of your job."

"I was going to do it, but now I might not be back until too late. Please, Sprig." A horn honks outside. "There they are!" She kisses Sprig on the head the way Mom does, and says, "*Please*, honey."

"Okay," Sprig says.

"Great!" Dakota zips up her jacket and pulls on her ski cap. "I have my cell, Sprig." She pats her jacket pocket. "You can always call me if you have any problems. You won't forget anything, will you? You won't forget to fill Cora's bowl with fresh water and take her out, and —"

"Dakota, if you say one more thing, I'm not going to do it." Sprig pushes her sister through the kitchen, into the glass-enclosed porch, and out the door. It's a perfect day for skiing, cold and clear. At the foot of the driveway, Krystee is leaning out the window of her mother's car. Dakota waves. "Here I come," she calls out and springs down the steps.

"Dakota," Sprig yells. "*Wait*. You forgot something." She can't help smirking as she hands over Dakota's skis.

A little after four that afternoon, Sprig is in Miss Ruthie's apartment, sweeping the kitchen floor, when Dakota walks in, her face shining. "Hi! I'm here," she says. "Where's Cora?" At the sound of her name, Cora, who's been lying on her rug near the heater, thumps her tail. "There you are!" Dakota cries. "Did Sprig take good care of you?"

"Yes, Sprig took good care of her," Sprig says. "Sprig walked Cora two times, once this morning and once this afternoon."

"Great!" Dakota beams as she peels off her jacket. "She did her business?"

"Yes, but she had a hard time pooping. And then she did it on someone's property, and it was kind of yucky."

Dakota sprawls into a chair. "Do I have to know all the details? That's so gross."

"It's not gross, Dakota, it's natural. I couldn't just leave it there. I wanted to just throw snow over it, but I thought that was cheating, so I cleaned it up with a plastic bag."

"Whatever," Dakota says, looking up at the ceiling and smiling.

Sprig's eyes follow Dakota's. What she sees is what she expects — the ceiling. "What is that weird look on your face?"

"Cora! Do I have a weird look on my face? Come on, tell me the truth." Cora lumbers to her feet and lies down near Dakota.

"Cora's worried about you," Sprig says. "She thinks you're weird."

"Is that what you think, doggy dog?" Dakota slings her feet onto Cora's back.

"Hey! Take your feet off Cora," Sprig says. "You're being disrespectful. Cora's old. Like Miss Ruthie. How do you think Miss Ruthie would feel if you put your feet on her and called her doggy dog?"

"Are you nuts? I would never do that. Anyway, Cora likes having my feet on her."

Sprig takes Cora's head in her hands. "Is that true, Cora?" She kisses the dog's nose.

"You like kissing her, don't you?" Dakota says, and that same peculiar smile crosses her face. She leans forward. "Want me to tell you a secret?"

"Take your feet off Cora, and you can tell me."

"But can I trust you?" She grabs Sprig's chin. "If I tell you, you have to promise not to tell anyone."

"Okay, I promise. What's the big secret?"

Dakota puckers up her lips and air-kisses Sprig. "I'll give you a hint. Thomas Buckthorn was at the ski lodge too."

"Okay, I get it! He followed you."

"Why would you think that?"

"Because he came here yesterday to find you."

"*What?* He didn't!"

"Yes, he did."

"Shut *up*! Thomas Buckthorn was here, right here?"

Sprig nods. "It was when I was shoveling the walk. He was on his cross-country skis. And he knew my name," she adds.

"Why didn't you call me?" Dakota pulls at

the little silver rings in her earlobes. "I can't believe this! Wait until I tell Krystee. You should have called me."

"Dakota. You were out walking Cora."

"Why didn't you tell me when I came home?"

"I don't know. I guess I forgot."

"Swear you're not making it up. This is really true, Sprig? On your honor?"

Sprig nods. "He skied over from his house, and then he asked me all these questions, like, did I like downhill or cross-country better."

"He asked *you* that? Why?"

Sprig shrugs. "Maybe he wanted me to go skiing with him."

"In your dreams, honey. What did he say about me?"

"He wanted to know if you like cross-country or downhill better."

"I hope you didn't say anything stupid."

"I told him I thought you liked both."

"Okay. That's okay." Dakota fiddles with her hair, piling it on top of her head, then letting it drop. "Which way do you like best?" she asks.

Sprig crosses her arms and considers. "You

look pretty both ways, but you look older when it's up."

"I do?" Holding her hair up, Dakota checks her reflection in the slightly spotted mirror on the wall. "Did Thomas say anything else about me?"

"Not really. I told him that you were working. I think he liked that."

"He's so cute," Dakota says. "I can't believe I was gone when he was here."

"But you saw him today," Sprig says. "So that makes it even."

"True, true." Dakota pushes aside Sprig's hair and speaks into her ear in a half whisper. "This is the secret. Thomas and I skied ahead of Krystee, and when we got over on the other side of the hill? *He kissed me.*" Dakota sits down and tilts back in the chair. "What do you think of *that!*"

13

THE GREEN
DISEASE

"**W**ELL, class," Mr. Julius says, unhinging himself from behind his desk and standing up, "I want to thank you all for your personal essays."

Sprig notices that he's wearing his orange tie again, the one with pumpkins on it, but somehow she doesn't mind as much as she did just a few days ago. So many other things seem more important, or maybe just one other thing — the news that Dad is going to Afghanistan.

"You're going to correct your essays right now, folks. I saw quite a few careless mistakes and a lot of misspelled words."

Is he looking at Sprig? She was in such a hurry when she copied over the essay Sunday night. Which seems like a thousand years ago. A thousand years before Mom told them about Dad and Afghanistan. Mr. Julius starts through the aisles, handing back the essays. When he gets to Russell, he says, "Skimpy on the details there, Russell. Your family in *four* lines?"

Sprig turns around. Russell is laughing along with everyone else. He grins at her and holds up four fingers, as if he's proud of his four-line essay.

"Class, one more thing before you start working," Mr. Julius says, as he goes back to his desk. "Any questions about what I wrote on your paper, consult the person sitting behind you."

Oh, terrific. That means Russell. But never mind, she's not going to ask him anything. Look what Mr. Julius wrote across the top of her paper: *Nicely done introduction to your family, Sprig.* She's pretty sure he didn't write that for Russell's skimpy four lines! She deflates a little as she looks at her essay and counts the number of misspelled words Mr. Julius circled in red. She's never been a super speller, but seven misspelled words at one blow might be a record. What was she thinking of when she wrote *lite*hearted? Dumb mistake. She corrects it. Next, *engeneer*, a totally careless mistake. Dad taught her to spell that word before she even knew what it meant. *Ridiculus* is another careless mistake — leaving out one letter in her haste to finish the paper. But what about *espechally, sereous, superor,* and *extremly?*

Russell taps her on the back. "Hey, Ewing. I'm done with mine. Six more sentences. You having any problems?" Without waiting for an answer, he peers over her shoulder. "Aha! I zee you have zee trouble with zee spelling."

"Russell, stop bothering me!" Sprig flaps her hand at him. "Go away." She has to concentrate. Is it *supperier?* Or *souperier?* Or neither?

Russell slides a note onto her desk.

To Sprig Ewing — This is a serious note. I am especially good at spelling. I hope you don't think I am acting superior for saying so. I am here to help you.
    Your extremely friendly speller, Russell Ezra-Evans

"That was so sweet of Russell," Bliss says, as they sit down in the cafeteria.

"I don't know why I'm such a bad speller," Sprig says. "I read, I read all the time, but I guess I don't look at the way words are spelled. I'm just reading them! I forget that they're even words. I'm just seeing the pictures that — oh, there's Russell now, coming straight for us."

"Hey there," Russell says, sitting down and opening his lunch bag. He takes out a plastic container full of salad.

"Is that all you're having for lunch?" Bliss asks.

"That's it. I'm trying to lose the flab. Did you see Mr. Julius's essay? He put it up on the bulletin board with a picture of his girlfriend. She's so hot. He writes all about her; his whole essay is just about her, practically. Mr. Julius is a cool guy."

"He's still not as good as Mrs. Foote," Sprig says loyally, although she hasn't thought about Mrs. Foote for many days now. "He's just the substitute. She's a real teacher."

Russell kicks her foot under the table. "Bad attitude, Ewing."

"Keep your feet to yourself, Ezra-Evans!"

"I read Mr. Julius's essay too," Bliss says. "His girlfriend's name is Megan. Wow, she's so pretty, and she's in the army, a helicopter pilot in Afghanistan. That is so cool."

"I don't think it's so cool," Sprig says. "Bliss! Afghanistan is dangerous."

"Well, she must be really brave," Bliss says, a little defensively.

"Like my dad," Sprig says.

"What does that mean?" Russell asks. "Your dad's not in the Army."

"Thanks for the information. My dad's going to Afghanistan to help build schools there." Sprig pushes away her food. She doesn't want to talk about it.

"I never want to be in the Army," Bliss says. "Anyway, I know I couldn't be a pilot. When we fly to Arizona to visit my grandfather? I can't even look out the window or I'll be sick!"

Russell gives his weird laugh, sort of like a seal barking. Bliss seems to like it, though. She laughs with him. Sprig sits back and watches as Russell digs into his pants pocket and brings out a crumpled piece of paper. His essay. "Look at this, Bliss," he says, "look at all the things Mr. Julius wrote about my essay."

"The famous four lines," Sprig says.

"*Now* the famous ten," Russell says. "I added stuff about my baby brother. He's five months old, and" — Russell forks up a chunk of raw broccoli, looks at it dolefully, then puts it in his mouth — "his name is Wheel."

"*Wheel?*" Sprig says.

"Clean your ears, Ewing. I said *Will*. Do you like that name?"

"I like it better than Wheel, Ezra-Evans."

"It was so fun writing about my family," Bliss says. "My dad has these math jokes that are sort of corny? But they break him up. I put in one for Mr. Julius. Question: Why was the six afraid of the seven?"

"Why?" Russell asks, obligingly.

"Because seven eight nine."

"Great joke," Russell says. He eyes Sprig's dessert, a double chocolate cupcake with chocolate frosting. "That cupcake looks pretty good."

"It's yummy, but you can't have any."

"Sprig!" Bliss says.

"Well, he's on a diet." Sprig pushes the cupcake across the table to Bliss. "But you aren't, have some. Come on," Sprig urges. "I know you love chocolate."

"Maybe just a sliver." Bliss cuts off a small slice.

Russell pulls the cupcake over to his side. "I'll have a sliver too. Man cannot live on broccoli alone," he says, popping a good-size chunk into his mouth. "Bliss, have some more," he says, as if it's his cupcake. He watches as she cuts another slice. "Good," he approves.

"It's for you," Bliss says, handing it to him. They smile at each other.

"My turn," Sprig says, taking back the cupcake. "Okay with you guys if I have a piece of my cupcake?"

It isn't the remains of her chocolate cupcake that Sprig broods over on the bus going home though, but that shared smile between Bliss and Russell. It doesn't seem fair! Dad is away, he's going to be sent to Afghanistan, and as if all that isn't bad enough, now her best friend is cozying up to — well, not her worst enemy, but the longest-running pest in her life! Her belly aches as if she's swallowed a tiny, sharp-toothed dog. Could this be . . . *jealousy*?

"Come on up, sweetheart," Miss Ruthie calls from her doorway, as Sprig is going up the driveway. "Where's your sister? I want you both to meet someone."

"Dakota went home with her girlfriend," Sprig says, stamping snow off her boots in Miss Ruthie's kitchen. She looks around, but she doesn't see anyone except Cora, who's lying under the table. "Who did you want me to meet?"

Miss Ruthie beckons her into the bedroom. Cora gets up and comes after Sprig, but Miss Ruthie won't let Cora in. She closes the bedroom door and says, "Now, Sprig, tell me what you see that's new in here."

Sprig looks around. There's Miss Ruthie's double bed with its lacy spread, there's the tall bureau with the long mirror above it and Miss Ruthie's comb and brush neatly laid out, and there's the wall covered with multiple pictures of Miss Ruthie's two nieces, and there's the window with — "Wow!" Sprig says. "Where did she come from?"

"He," Miss Ruthie corrects. "Don't insult my new friend."

The *he* is a skin-and-bones, black-and-white-checkered cat sitting on the windowsill and staring at Sprig with a distinctly unfriendly look.

"He's been showing up on my porch for the past week," Miss Ruthie says. "I've been feeding him and checking the 'lost cat' ads, but look how skinny he is, poor thing. I'm sure someone abandoned him." She presses her lips together. "He's not going to go hungry again!"

"What's his name?"

"Plucky, because he's a survivor. Oh, don't try to pet him," she warns as Sprig approaches the cat. "He's a wary fellow, he still doesn't even trust me. Look at him! He knows everything we're saying."

"Does Cora like him?" Sprig asks.

"Oh, Cora! She's jealous as can be. You should hear her! She *growls* at Plucky. Now when did you ever hear Cora growl?" Miss Ruthie laughs. "Oh, she's got the green disease all right."

Jealousy again! And why shouldn't Cora be jealous, Sprig thinks later, going down the steps. After all, Cora was Miss Ruthie's friend *first* — as Bliss was hers.

14

A SECURITY THING

SPRIG and Dakota are sprawled out on Mom's bed, watching a movie. Mom is supposed to be watching with them but, in reality, she's only half watching. Every once in a while, she looks up from the book she's reading and catches up with the movie.

"Mom," Dakota says, when the movie is over. "Look, it's almost ten o'clock and Dad hasn't called. Do you think he's in a meeting again? Do you think he'll call you later, like that other time?"

Mom closes her book. "Put the DVD in its case, Sprig, and bring it out to the hall table, so I remember to return it. Dakota, you take the popcorn bowl into the kitchen and wash it.

And then both of you come back in here. I have something I need to tell you."

Sprig shuffles slowly into the hall. Her stomach is beginning to hurt, and she knows it isn't too much popcorn. It's those words again: *something I need to tell you.* Sprig puts the DVD on the little round table, then suddenly sits down on the floor with her back against the wall. She's going to sit right here. She's not going back in Mom's bedroom. She doesn't want to hear what Mom *needs* to tell her. She doesn't have to hear it either. She won't listen, anyway. She just won't!

But, of course, she does. She goes back in the bedroom. She perches on the edge of the bed. And she hears what Mom has to say. Dad is on his way, this very moment, to Afghanistan. Even while they were watching that stupid movie, he was leaving them.

"We didn't even get to say good-bye to him," Sprig chokes out.

"I know," Mom says, "and he felt really bad about that, but it's a security thing. It could be dang —" She cuts herself off. "It's better that he just goes this way, quietly, and does his work, and then —"

"What about phone calls?" Dakota says. "We're not going to talk to him again until he comes home?"

"No, no, no," Mom says. "As soon as he gets settled, he'll start calling us. He'll call us every night, the way he always does."

"How can he do that?" Sprig cries. "He'll be in *Afghanistan*."

"They have very good cell phone service," Mom says. "It's not going to be a problem." She gathers both girls to her. "I want you to remember that your father will be coming home to us in a month or so. A lot of dads won't be doing that anytime soon."

"That's true," Dakota says. "A girl in my class, Mellissa Katter, her father was in Iraq, and —"

"Don't tell me about it," Sprig says. "I know about her, it's too sad."

For once, Dakota doesn't argue with her,

but now Sprig is remembering how her class wrote a sympathy letter to Mellissa and her family, and how her father's picture was in the *Alliance Post Herald.* All along, the newspaper had been printing pictures of the soldiers killed in Iraq, but this was the first time Sprig knew someone connected to one of those men.

In the middle of the night, Sprig wakes, her heart thrumming in her throat. She can't find him. She's been running down one dark street after another, looking for Dad, looking for him everywhere, and not finding him. *She can't find him anywhere.*

Before she registers that she's awake, she's across the room, pulling at her sister's blankets. "Dakota, Dakota . . ." Sprig climbs onto Dakota's bed. She's shivering, shaking, still running down those desolate streets, still looking into dark doorways and empty alleys. "What's happening?" she cries. "What's happening with Dad? Where is he?"

"Hey, hey, hey." Dakota sits up. She stares

at Sprig, then, her voice still sleep-clogged, she says, "You want to sleep with me?"

Without answering, Sprig scrambles under the covers and wraps herself around Dakota's back. Her sister's hair is in her face; it smells good, spicy. Sprig breathes in the smell, holds on to her sister, and in a moment, she's asleep.

15

I THOUGHT
YOU MIGHT WANT
TO KNOW

"**MR. JULIUS,**" Sprig says, standing by his desk.

"Yes, Sprig?" He doesn't look up from the form he's filling out.

"My father —" She stops, clutching her books to her chest. "My dad," she starts again. "Um, I thought you might want to know —" She glances at the bulletin board with the picture of Megan McKenna, the helicopter pilot, still pinned on it. She is so pretty, sitting at the controls, safety glasses pushed up on her forehead, smiling into the camera, as if it's Sunday in the park and she's off for a picnic. You wouldn't know from looking that the picture was taken in Afghanistan.

"What is it, Sprig?" Mr. Julius makes a mark on the form, then puts down his pen. "What can I do for you?"

"My father's in Afghanistan."

Mr. Julius looks up. Now she has all his attention. "I didn't realize your father was an Army man."

Sprig shakes her head. "He isn't. Remember my essay? He's an engineer and an architect, and he's there to consult about building schools. For everyone. I mean, schools for girls too. You know they wouldn't let girls go to school, I mean those people, the Taliban, and my father says the schools he's going to build, they will definitely admit girls." The words pour out. "When he went there, I mean, when he flew over last week, it was Friday, and we were watching a movie, and my sister and I didn't even know he was gone. He couldn't tell us, it was a security thing."

"I understand," Mr. Julius says. "So how long will he be gone, Sprig?"

"Too long," she blurts.

"How long is that?"

"I don't know exactly. Last night when he called, he said it could be six weeks or even two months."

"That probably does seem like a long time to you."

"It *is* a long time," Sprig says, and then, checking herself, she asks politely, "When will Miss McKenna be home?"

Mr. Julius drums his fingers on the desk. "Not for another year. Actually fourteen months."

"Oh! Why is she going to be away so long?"

"Lieutenant McKenna signed up for another tour," Mr. Julius says. "She felt it was her duty."

"Oh," Sprig says again. Fourteen months! "Mr. Julius." She leans forward. "Maybe she can come home sooner. Maybe things will change there, and they'll send her home."

"That's a good thought, Sprig. I'll hold on to it." He looks up at the clock. "You better go back to your desk now."

As soon as she sits down, Sprig leans over to Bliss and whispers, "I told him about my dad being in Afghanistan. I was stupid to say anything! His girlfriend isn't going to be home for *fourteen months*. He probably hates me now."

"Oh, please! I do not agree!" Bliss grabs Sprig's arm. "You wanted to tell someone about your dad —"

"Well, why didn't I just tell you?"

"Because I already know, dodo! Maybe Mr. J. was happy to talk to someone about his girl-friend," Bliss whispers. "I bet he was really glad someone else understands."

"That's a good thought," Sprig says. "I'll hold on to it."

16

THOSE DOG TEETH AGAIN

"**PEOPLE!**" Mr. Julius calls. "Will everyone please pay attention?" He raps on his desk. "Russell has an announcement to make. Bliss and Sprig, could you two quiet down? I know it's Friday, but we need to stay on task, people. We still have work to cover today. Okay, Russell, you're on."

Russell pulls his shirt straight, clasps his hands, and bows. "You're all invited to a party at my house Sunday night, starting at five P.M.," Russell says in his deep voice. "In fact, the whole school is invited, 'cause of my sister, Lara, who's in Sprig's sister's class." He points two fingers at Sprig, and everyone turns and looks at her. "It's Lara's birthday. She's going to be thirteen. There'll be lots of food — stuff kids like, not real healthy stuff, so don't worry." Everybody laughs, and Russell takes another bow. "*My* parents say be sure to tell *your* parents that *my* parents will both be present, so *your* parents don't think it's some wild, unsupervised, party-animal thing." More laughter. Another bow. "And you're invited too, Mr. Julius."

"Thank you, Russell," Mr. Julius says. "Okay, everybody —"

"Mr. Julius —" Russell puts up his hand. "I have something else to say, okay?"

"All right, Russell, but let's make it snappy."

"Well, besides being Lara's birthday, it's also a sort of winterfest party to celebrate the new year, that's what my dad says, even though it's already February, but we don't always do things on time in our family, plus my mom says it's to be happy that we've made it safely through last year and this year so far."

"Amen," Mr. Julius says, and he turns for a moment to look at the picture on the bulletin board.

• • •

"The way Russell just gets up in front of everybody and talks and is so, so *all together*," Bliss says later, as she and Sprig walk toward her bus. Sprig is staying overnight with Bliss. "I mean, he doesn't stumble or anything. I don't think I could do that. I know I couldn't."

"Oh, that's just Russell. You know how he is. He's a show-off."

"I do not agree," Bliss says. "You don't give him enough credit, Sprig. It's a talent, what he does. I think he's great."

"You know what, Bliss, you never agree with anything I say." Sprig means that to be funny, but it doesn't come out that way.

Bliss looks at her and shrugs. "It's my dad's turn to cook tonight," she says, after a moment. "Are you prepared for falafel?"

"What's that?"

"It's this stuff made from chickpeas that you put on pita. You'll see. It's really good. Russell loves it."

"When was that?" Sprig says. "Why didn't I know?"

"Know *what*?"

"When did Russell eat at your house?"

"He didn't," Bliss says.

"You just said —"

"All I said was —"

"Never mind! I can see what's going on." Those sharp dog teeth are snagged in Sprig's belly, and the words tumble out before she can stop them. Maybe she doesn't want to stop them. "You like Russell better than you like me. I see the way you look at him."

They're standing face-to-face, Sprig's hot face up close to Bliss's hot face. "How do I look at him?" Bliss says. "I mean, besides with my eyes?"

"*Adoringly*," Sprig says. "You laugh at everything he says, and you ask him about things you know better than he does. You act stupid on purpose around him, just so he'll be your friend!"

Bliss takes a step back. "I act *stupid*? Is that what you think? Well, let me tell you something, Sprig Ewing. You were right the other day, when you said *you* were dumb to tell Mr. Julius about your father and get him all upset. It was really dumb, a really dumb, dumb, *dumb* thing to do."

"If that's the way you feel," Sprig gets out, "maybe you don't want me to come home with you."

"Maybe I don't," Bliss says.

Sprig turns and, without another word, stomps off toward her bus, kicking lumps of snow aside.

"What happened?" Dakota says, when she sees Sprig getting on the bus. She's already seated with Krystee. "I thought you were going home with —"

"Nothing happened," Sprig says. "I don't want to talk about it."

17

NINE
ONE ONE

"**ARE** you sure you don't want to go shopping with Dakota and me?" Mom says Saturday afternoon, as they're finishing lunch.

"I'm sure," Sprig says. She doesn't feel *at all* like shopping. She doesn't feel like doing anything. It's the fight-with-Bliss thing, plus Dad didn't call them last night, and now she's having all kinds of worried thoughts.

"Well, what are you going to do this afternoon?" Mom asks.

Sprig doesn't know what she's going to do, she only knows she doesn't want to trail after Dakota! If things weren't all messed up, she and Bliss would be together, talking about Russell's party tomorrow night. "Maybe I'll just take a nap," she says.

"I hope you're not getting sick." Mom puts her hand on Sprig's forehead. "No fever, that's good." She looks at her watch. "Dakota, go get ready, hon. The stores are going to be jammed if we go too late."

"I am ready," Dakota says.

"I think you should change your shirt."

"You don't like this one?" Dakota looks down at her pink blouse.

"I don't like it," Sprig says. "I don't like that color with your red hair."

"I don't like your ten-year-old opinion."

"The shirt's nice," Mom says, "and the color is fine for you, but it has too many buttons. It'll be a nuisance when you want to try things on. Didn't I get you one just like that, Sprig?"

Sprig nods. "Mom," she says, once Dakota goes to change, "do you remember what I told you last night?"

Mom has all her credit cards out on the table and is sorting through them. "What, honey? Ah, here it is, the one I was looking for."

"Mom." Sprig's throat is tight. "Bliss and I had a fight."

"Oh, right. I'm sorry, honey. Don't brood over it, okay?" She's putting all her cards back into her purse now. "I'm sure the two of you will make up."

"Mom, I'm ready," Dakota says. She's changed into a green pullover.

Sprig stands at the window and watches as Mom backs down the driveway. Outside, the sky is gray, and wind whirls the snow up into flurries. Inside, the house is quiet, except for the rumble of the furnace. "Good," she says out loud. "They're gone." But at once she feels lonely and presses her forehead against the cold window.

What now? She could do her vacation homework and get it out of the way. She could clean up her side of her room. She could think about what she'll wear to Russell's party tomorrow night. No, none of that.

She goes on the computer and plays solitaire and bores herself. She eats chocolate ice cream out of the carton, and it's too cold and makes her sinuses ache. She punches in Bliss's number on the phone, but as soon as she hears the ring, she hangs up. Finally, she puts on her boots and her fleece, crosses the yard, and goes up the stairs to Miss Ruthie's apartment.

The door is locked. Sprig knocks and calls, "Miss Ruthie, it's me!"

When Miss Ruthie opens the door, Sprig is shocked to see that she's still in her old blue bathrobe. She squints at Sprig, almost as if she doesn't know her. Her gray hair is wild, uncombed. "What's the matter, Miss Ruthie? Are you sick?"

"I don't know." Miss Ruthie's voice is slurred, like she's *drunk* or something. "Sprig..." Her voice falls away. "Come...in." She sits down abruptly at the kitchen table, pressing her hands slowly to her neck. "I'm a...I'm...dizzy."

Cora whines and puts her head in Miss Ruthie's lap. "Oh...don't," Miss Ruthie breathes, as if she can hardly get out the words.

"Come here, Cora," Sprig says. "Miss Ruthie, do you want me to call the doctor?"

Slowly, she shakes her head. "No...no...it'll pass," she says, in the same slurred voice. She rises and shuffles unsteadily toward her bedroom, holding on to the wall. She makes it to the side of her bed, then just stands there, swaying.

"You better lie down," Sprig says anxiously. "Do you want me to cover you up?" She pulls up the quilt, tucking it around the old woman's shoulders.

"Cora . . ." Miss Ruthie says, her voice fading. "Foo . . ." Her eyes close.

"What about Cora, Miss Ruthie?" The old woman doesn't answer. She's breathing heavily.

In the kitchen, Sprig sees that both Plucky's and Cora's food bowls are in the sink, along with some dishes and pots. "Cora, did you get fed or not?" Sprig takes a can of dog food from the cupboard. At the sound of the can opener, Cora comes over, sits down expectantly, and grins at Sprig.

"Gotcha," Sprig says. She fills the food bowls and the water bowls, and calls Plucky, who slinks into sight from behind a chest of drawers. While the animals are eating, Sprig punches in Mom's cell number. What she gets is Mom's mailbox. "Please leave a message. . . ."

"Mom, Miss Ruthie's sick. She has a virus or

something," Sprig says. "She really doesn't feel good, I mean she looks terrible, Mom, and she's in bed now, and I'm taking care of Cora and Plucky and —" She pauses for breath. "The thing is, she doesn't want me to call the doctor, but do you think I should call anyway? Who is her doctor, Mom? Do you know? Call me back when you get this message. Miss Ruthie is sleeping, and I don't want to wake her up. Call me! Okay?"

Cora has eaten all her food and is sitting down near Plucky, who's still picking at his food. "Go ahead, it's okay," Sprig says to the cat. "Cora's not going to eat your food, even if she is looking at it like that."

Sprig sits down at the table and tries to think what to do next. She's sure she shouldn't leave Miss Ruthie alone, but shouldn't she do something else? Why isn't Dad here! He would know what to do. She goes to the bedroom and tiptoes over to the bed. Miss Ruthie is lying there, her mouth open. Her skin is damp and she looks really, really pale.

When Sprig is sick, Mom brings her magazines to read, and lets her lie on the couch and watch TV and eat special food, like baby pear sauce. None of that is any good for Miss Ruthie, so Sprig straightens the newspaper on the table next to her bed, centers the little lamp with its bluebird lampshade, and checks to make sure the window is tightly closed. Miss Ruthie's black lace-up shoes are in the middle of the floor next to a crumpled pair of slacks, as if she tried to get dressed and couldn't. Sprig hangs up the slacks and puts the shoes in the closet. Then she tiptoes out.

In the kitchen, she watches Cora and Plucky, who both watch her. Cora plants herself directly in front of Sprig and gazes at her with half-blind eyes. "What?" Sprig says. "You want me to do something else? What, Cora? You want me to wash the dishes? Okay, I'll do them."

She runs hot water in the sink and thinks about how she'll tell Dad this whole story when he calls later. He *will* call later, won't he? "He will, he will, he will, he will call," she says out loud, but quietly. "Yes, he will," she tells herself again, placing another clean dish carefully in the rack. After she finishes washing the pots, she tiptoes back into the bedroom. Miss Ruthie hasn't moved. Her breathing is thick and rapid, as if she's gasping for each breath.

Sprig dials her mother's cell again, punching the numbers in hard.

"Please leave a message. . . ."

"Mom! Why don't you have the cell phone on? Why aren't you answering? Call me!" Nearly an hour has passed since she called the first time. "Mom, hurry up and call me. Please!"

Who else could she ask for advice? Bliss? *No.* What about Mr. Julius? "That's a good idea," she says out loud. She finds the phone book on the bottom shelf of one of the cupboards. She peels away the thin pages, looking for his name. She finds M. Jukes and Patryk July, but no Thomas Julius.

"What do I do now? What do I do now?" She paces back and forth, peeks into the bedroom again, then looks out the kitchen window and across the field, where she saw Thomas Buckthorn skiing away on that other Saturday. If he were here now, she would even ask *him* what to do.

She cartwheels across the kitchen, just to do *something*. When she stands up, Cora is gazing at her again. Sprig kisses the dog. "You're really worried too, aren't you? Do you want me to call the doctor, Cora? I don't know her name! I could call 911, but that's for emergencies." She looks into Cora's eyes. "What if it's just a cold or something ordinary like that, wouldn't it be stupid of me to call, Cora?"

Sprig sits down on the floor and puts her arms around the dog's neck. "I know what you're thinking. You're thinking what if it's something really bad, like the Ebola virus, the one that kills you. That's what you're thinking, isn't it, Cora?"

Cora keeps her blurred gaze on Sprig. *Yes*, she's saying, *that's exactly what I'm thinking*. Sprig stands, goes to the phone, and punches in the three numbers.

18

SOON AS
I CAN

"**AND** last, on the six o'clock news report, we have a story of a young girl saving the life of one of our senior citizens with her quick thinking," Bob Engelhard, the evening news anchor, says.

"Oh my god," Dakota cries. "They're talking about you, Sprig. Mom! Come in here," she calls. "Sprig is on the news."

Mom sits down on the arm of the couch, just as Bob Engelhard turns to Mary Roman, his coanchor, and says, "Mary, fill us in."

"It's a pleasure, Bob. We have so many downbeat stories, but not this one!" Mary looks into the Ewings' living room. "This afternoon, ten-year-old Grace Ewing had the presence of mind to call in the emergency folks, when her seventy-eight-year-old neighbor, Ruth Levin, became ill."

"Oh, no," Sprig says, covering her face. "This is so embarrassing."

"You're famous," Dakota says. "My sister's famous! Maybe they're going to show your picture."

Sure enough, Sprig's class picture from last year —"I look so young," she cries — flashes on the screen, followed by a picture of their house, then the garage, and Miss Ruthie's windows, and the little porch.

"Grace was alone with the elderly woman and had no idea that Ms. Levin was the victim of a stroke," Mary is saying. Now the camera shows the exterior of Memorial Hospital and then the red EMERGENCY ROOM sign. "Doctor Raymond, a heart specialist, told this reporter that time is of the essence in strokes." Mary turns to Bob, and he picks up the narrative.

"Mary, had the Ewing girl — she's only ten years old, isn't that amazing? — had she not acted so rapidly, Ms. Levin might have been seriously incapacitated for the rest of her life."

"I know, Bob. There's got to be some grateful people out there tonight. As it is, her chances for recovery are very good. I was reading something the other day about this being the Me Generation. I don't think so!"

"I should say not," Bob says. "And now, let's look at the weather, Mary. . . ."

"Wow," Dakota says. "My little sister is a hero."

Sprig sags against the back of the couch. Everybody says they're so proud of her: Mom and the doctors at the hospital, and now the six o'clock news. But what Sprig keeps thinking is that she let too much time pass before she called 911. She waited to see if Miss Ruthie felt better, she waited for Mom to call her back, she fiddled around looking for Mr. Julius's phone number. She waited too long. The moment she saw Miss Ruthie swaying in the door, uncombed, still in her bathrobe, she should have known something was wrong.

They're all telling her she saved Miss Ruthie from having a lot more damage. *Damage.* It sounds like a caved-in car, like a house smashed by a hurricane, like Miss Ruthie covered with tubes and wires and so sick they won't let anyone in to see her for more than a minute.

Later that evening when Dad calls, Mom tells him the whole story — everything, including that Sprig was on the evening news. "Your dad wants to talk to you now, Sprig," she says.

"Me, first?" Sprig glances at Dakota.

"Go ahead," Dakota says. "You deserve it. This time," she adds.

Sprig takes the phone into the other room. "Hi, Dad."

"Sprig," Dad says. "I'm so proud of you for your quick thinking."

"Dads." Sprig leans in to the phone. "I waited too long to call."

"Sprig, you saved Miss Ruthie's life. It could have been a whole lot worse."

"I guess so," she says. "But what if there's *damage* and it's my fault because I —"

"Sprig." His voice deepens. "I want you to listen carefully. I want you to hear this, all the way from Kabul, Afghanistan, to Alliance, New York. You can't second-guess yourself. Sometimes we only get one chance, and then we live with what we choose to do or not do. What you did was a good thing, and we're all lucky — Miss Ruthie is very lucky! She's lucky that you were there. Do you hear what I'm saying?"

"Yes," Sprig says after a moment. "I hear you, Dad." And then she asks the question she always asks. "Are you coming home soon?"

And he gives the answer he always gives. "Soon as I can. Soon as my work is done."

19

HELLO AND
GOOD-BYE

LIGHTS sparkle in every window of the sprawling Ezra-Evans house. Dakota is out of the car almost before Mom stops, but Sprig lingers. "Mom," she says, "you know what I wish? I wish I'd stayed home. Bliss is going to be here at the party," she explains.

"Well, honey, there's only one thing to do. Make up with her," Mom says, as if there's nothing to it. "It's never as hard as you think. The longer you wait, the harder it'll be. I'll be here at ten to pick you both up," she adds, as Sprig finally gets out of the car.

Russell's parents, two tall, smiling people, greet her at the door. Inside, Dakota has already taken off her boots and is putting on her black ballet slippers. She's wearing black tights and a new glitter tee shirt, and her hair is piled on top of her head. Spurts of music, talk, and laughter pour out of the living room.

Sprig hangs up her jacket in the jammed closet and kicks off her boots, then realizes she forgot to bring her sneakers. "Oh, no! Dakota, what should I do?"

Her sister looks at Sprig's dog-patterned socks and shrugs. "Doesn't matter. Your socks are cute."

"Are you sure it's okay? It doesn't look too weird?"

"It's fine!" She gives Sprig a push toward the living room. "Lighten up, this is going to be fun. Do I look okay?" She fingers the tiny silver hoops in her ears.

Sprig nods. "You look —" She's about to say "beautiful," but Dakota has spotted Krystee and run off.

The living room is huge, crowded, and hot. A pool table is set up in front of the two long windows, and in the group around it, Sprig sees Bliss and Russell, side-by-side. Big Russell in a white shirt and a red tie, and tiny Bliss in a red blouse and white skirt. What did they do, color-coordinate their clothes? A funny thought, only Sprig isn't laughing. It's Russell and Bliss who are laughing, who are having fun together. Who *are* together. Sprig's legs quiver, as if she's outside in the cold, cold air. She *is* outside. Out in the cold.

Dimly, she remembers the stupid quarrel with Bliss, and then she remembers that other moment when their friendship almost foundered. She'd saved the day that time, and it hadn't been hard. She'd thrown her arms around Bliss and hugged her. Was that all it would take now to bring her in from the cold?

"'Scuse me." Sprig pushes through the crowd toward Bliss. She has gone only a few steps, when Bliss turns around, looks across the room, and — what is it they say in the stories Sprig reads? — *their eyes lock.* Yes, that's it. Sprig's eyes and Bliss's lock. Then Bliss unlocks them. She spins around and says something to Russell that makes him laugh out loud. That big barking-seal laugh of Russell's — at her? — is like a wind blowing Sprig out of the living room, across the hall, and into another room.

"Close the door," someone calls to her. A group of kids are clustered near the fireplace. They're chanting and counting. "Go, go, go ... thirty-three ... thirty-four ... go, go, go ... thirty-five ... thirty-six ..." Sprig moves closer and sees Thomas Buckthorn in the center of the group, kissing a girl Sprig recognizes as Amanda Griggs. Amanda is one of Dakota's classmates, and she's kissing Thomas back with unmistakable enthusiasm. If only Sprig had the nerve to say what she's thinking! *Stop that, Thomas Buckthorn. Stop that right now. You kissed my sister. You're supposed to be her boyfriend.*

"... forty-six ... forty-seven ..."

"Go for a minute," somebody urges. "Break the record." But a moment later, Amanda pulls away from Thomas, fanning her face. Thomas grins and pretends to stagger.

"Girl number six for fifty-one seconds," a boy cries out like a sports announcer. "Who's going to be the lucky number seven? Who's going to go for the minute record?" His eyes land on Sprig. "Hey, cute little socks girl, come on over here and try your luck."

"No, thanks," Sprig says, backing away. "Seven isn't my lucky number."

She hears the laughter as she ducks into yet another room, where food is featured, two long tables full of food. She quickly eats five tiny hot dogs, each one impaled with a colored tooth-pick, and drinks two glasses of punch. Now she's calmer. Food is always calming.

"Whew," she says softly, and puts a handful of chocolate kisses in her pocket for later.

Someone hip-bumps her. It's Russell. "You like chocolate kisses?" he asks.

"I'm not stealing them," she says.

"I like chocolate . . . *kisses* too." He smirks.

Oh, what is it with boys tonight? "I like anything chocolate," Sprig says, pretending she doesn't notice the smirk. "I never saw you wear-ing a tie before."

"Do you like it?"

She surveys him. "It looks good. And you got your hair cut too."

Russell puts his hand on his head. "My dad took the clippers to me. He says he always wanted to be a barber, not a lawyer. Maybe I'll wear the tie to school," he adds.

"I didn't say it looked *that* good," Sprig says. "So, how many rooms are there in this house, anyway?"

"Counting   bathrooms . . . lemme   see . . . fourteen."

"That's a lot," she says.

"Uh-huh. You want to see the upstairs?"

She shrugs. "Sure."

"Are you having a good time?" he asks, leading the way up the wide winding staircase.

"Uh, sure," she says. "I guess so."

He stops on the landing halfway up, and Sprig sits down on the window seat below the triangular stained-glass window. If she lived in this house, this would be where she'd come to read and daydream. "I like your house. This window is cool."

"My dad calls this house The Barn."

"That's funny, it's nothing like a barn."

"Except it's big."

"But so are you all," she says.

"Yeah, supersize." He sits down next to her. "That's what you call me, isn't it?"

Sprig's face heats up. "Maybe. Sometimes."

"I don't care. Like my dad says, people are going to say things, and if you care or don't care, it doesn't mean anything to them, so you might as well not care."

"That makes sense," Sprig says.

"My dad's got a really responsible job. I mean, not to boast or anything, but he's sort of important and, still, people he doesn't even know will come right up to him and ask, 'How's the air up there?' and stupid things like that."

Sprig looks down at her feet. Was calling Russell 'supersize' one of those stupid things? Probably. "I don't call you that anymore," she says.

"How come you're just wearing socks?" He swings his booted foot into her foot.

"Hey, that hurts! You always do things like that, and you know what," she says, surprising herself — she hadn't planned to say this — "I'm really sick of it."

"I always do things like what?" Russell says.

"Like hitting me and pinching me. And shoving. You just don't leave me alone. You've been doing that stuff since forever."

"What? I don't hit you!" Russell looks at her, his eyes bulging. "I hit you?" he says, as if the idea is brand-new and astonishing, and he gives a kind of sickly laugh, a laugh so un-Russell-like, so, well, *pathetic*, that Sprig takes pity on him.

"The good thing is, you haven't done it in a while," she says. "Maybe you're reforming, but you just had a slip. You forgot, right?"

"Forgot what?" he says.

"Not to hit me, bozo!" She claps him on the side of the head.

"Wait a second. You just hit me."

"Well, I didn't mean to," Sprig says. "But, anyway, that's a reminder never to hit me again. Got it? And here's another reminder," she says, and with both hands she shoves him off the window seat.

Russell looks up at her from the floor. "You know what?" He grins. "I like you."

Wooof. Wooof. . . . The little dog barks softly

in her ear, *More than Bliss?* Sprig holds out her hand to Russell. "Help?"

"Nope." He jumps up. And then he kisses her, first on her left cheek, then on her right cheek. He smells like chewing gum.

"Whoa," Sprig says. "What's that?"

"Don't you know? That's the way the French and Italians say hello and good-bye."

"Hello and good-bye," Sprig repeats, trying to decide if she hated those kisses — or liked them. "Well, which is it? Hello or good-bye?"

"Guess," Russell says.

20

HOW THE WALL
CAME DOWN

RUSSELL Ezra-Evans kissed Sprig, and this is too strange, almost too *delicious* to keep to herself. She doesn't know how she feels about those kisses, but she has to tell someone! As she runs, almost tumbles, down the stairs, giddy from the kisses, the thought of Bliss passes through her mind. Bliss, who won't even look at her.

She could tell Dakota, but as sure as the sun rises in the morning, Dakota would tell Krystee. In the crowded living room she checks out the kids dancing, the girls off in a corner singing, and a group on the couch doing a sudoku puzzle. No one looks reliable enough to tell.

"Isn't this party cool?" Mandy Halverson says. She's a plump blond girl who's always talking in class. She holds out a pack of gum. "Don't you hope Russell's parents do this every year?"

Sprig looks at Mandy's open blue eyes. Mandy's here, she's ready, she's listening. "Russell was showing me the house," Sprig begins.

"It's great, isn't it? Guess who I saw dancing real tight? You'll never guess!" She squeezes Sprig's arm, names two of the kids in their class, and darts off to tell someone else.

As the music stops and the floor clears a little, Sprig sees Bliss across the room talking to a girl who towers over her — Russell's sister, Lara, the birthday girl. Is Bliss telling her how nasty, mean, and *jealous* Sprig can be? It's all true. It's also true that it hasn't been much more than forty-eight hours since they had their fight, but it's been as lonely as forty-eight *days*. "Enough is enough," Sprig says out loud. That fight was her own fault. She started it, and now she's going to end it. "'Scuse me, 'scuse me." She moves through the crowd of kids milling around waiting for the next dance song. Her eyes are on Bliss. She's on a mission. First, make up with Bliss. No need for words. Just give her a hug, the way she did that afternoon when they had the almost-fight. Next, say something corny to make Bliss laugh, like *Fancy meeting you here, my dear.* Then say you're sorry. After that, tell about the kisses. And after that — well, *whatever.*

Just then, Lara moves off, and Bliss turns and sees Sprig. Bliss nods and raises her chin. Somehow, it doesn't feel like the right moment for a hug.

What is it the right moment for? Surely not the next thing that comes out of Sprig's mouth. "Are you hungry? I'm starved!" Maybe it's those kisses, or maybe it's all these emotions, but she's still ravenous and, although this isn't a very promising make-up line, she marches right on with food information. "The little hot dogs are really good. I ate five of them."

"I don't like hot dogs," Bliss says.

Sprig digs her hands into her pockets and comes out with the chocolates kisses she'd tucked away. Maybe it's a sign. *Kisses.* A stand-in for the hug? She offers them on her open hand to Bliss. "Chocolate kisses?"

Bliss's face says *No*, but her hand doesn't agree. Her hand takes one kiss, hovers as if it's going to take another, then moves away. Delicately, Bliss picks open the silver foil. Delicately, she puts the chocolate in her mouth. "Have another one," Sprig urges.

"Mmm, I don't think so," Bliss says. Her voice is like a wall.

Not a very big wall, but still, one that Sprig has to climb. She takes a breath. "The other day? In the parking lot? I shouldn't have said those things."

"No, you shouldn't," Bliss says. "But . . . I said things too."

Sprig holds out the rest of the chocolate kisses. "Three for you and two for me."

"Three for me?" Bliss says. "That's not exactly fair."

"Yes, it is, because I started things."

"Oh," Bliss says, and then she says, "Oh!" again, takes the three chocolate kisses, peels them, and puts them all in her mouth.

Sprig peels the last two kisses and puts them in her mouth. They give each other chocolate-flavored smiles and, just like that, the wall is down. They're friends again. "So!" Sprig says. "I have something interesting to tell you."

Before she can say another word, tall Lara Ezra-Evans is hurrying toward her, calling her name. "Sprig! Sprig! Your sister doesn't feel good. I think she's sick or something."

"Dakota?" Sprig hastily wipes her mouth. "What do you mean? What's wrong with her?"

"I don't know," Lara says. "I went in the kitchen for a glass of water, and she was in there, crying, and she wouldn't talk to me."

"Dakota was *crying*?"

"I know," Lara says. "That's not like Dakota. You better go talk to her. You better go right away."

21

THE
STINKER

IN the kitchen, Sprig and Bliss look around, but they don't see Dakota anywhere. It's not that the kitchen is dark — in fact, just the opposite, the light is almost too much. It bounces off two gleaming refrigerators, a huge stove covered with dials, and a long, shining stainless-steel table.

"She's not here," Sprig says. "Didn't Lara say —" She breaks off, as she sees her sister. Dakota is huddled under the table, her arms wrapped around her legs, her face buried on her knees, and her shoulders shaking. "Dakota!" Sprig cries. "What are you doing! Are you sick? Do you want me to call Mom?"

"Don't," Dakota says in a muffled voice.

"Don't what?"

"Don't talk to me!"

Sprig looks at Bliss, who opens her hands in a helpless, don't-ask-me-what-to-do gesture.

"Dakota," Sprig says, bending down to her sister, "whatever it is that's making you feel bad, it'll look better in the morning, and then you'll deal with it."

"Don't talk like Mom," Dakota chokes out. "You're just a kid, you don't understand. You don't understand anything," she cries. "Leave me alone, I hate you. I hate everybody."

Sprig stands up. "Suit yourself," she says. She tried, didn't she? It's not her fault if her sister is stubborn as a donkey. She motions to Bliss, and they go out and close the door behind them.

"What a stinker," Bliss says. She squeezes Sprig's arm. "Am I ever glad she's not my sister."

It's weird what happens next. Sprig practically yanks her arm free of Bliss's hand. Bliss's *clutching* hand is what she thinks, although, even as she thinks it, she knows it's totally unfair. Still, what gives Bliss the right to say those things about Dakota? Not that Sprig doesn't say the same things and lots worse, but that's different. Dakota is *her* sister, she can say whatever she wants about her. She can imagine baking Dakota into a cookie or sending her off on an ice floe forever, but that doesn't mean Bliss should do it. At least, not without Sprig's permission.

"You okay?" Bliss says, peering into Sprig's face.

"I guess so. You know what I was just thinking, Bliss? That ten ways thing I did, the list?"

Bliss smiles. "That was so fun."

"Actually . . . it was kind of juvenile," Sprig says. "Don't you think it was kind of juvenile?"

"Maybe," Bliss says, "but I liked it. I thought it was funny and cute. It was really cute. You thought so too," she adds.

Sprig turns and looks back at the closed kitchen door, and for a moment she thinks she can hear Dakota crying. That's when it hits her. Dakota's in the kitchen under the table. Something is definitely wrong, and what did Sprig do? She walked out on her sister, just left her there?

22

ONE FOR THE EYES AND ONE FOR THE NOSE

SPRIG kneels down to talk to Dakota, who's still under the table. "Dakota, can you tell me why you're crying?"

Dakota lifts a blotchy face. "You can't help me," she chokes. "Nobody can help me."

"Did you hurt yourself?"

"Nooo."

"Did someone say something mean to you?"

"Nooo."

"Can you tell me what happened?"

"Nooo."

"Are you sure you can't tell me? I know I'm being a pest, but —"

"Yess!"

"Yes I'm being a pest, or yes you can tell me?"

"Stop, stop talking, stop talking so much!

I'll tell you. I'll tell you what happened! I saw Thomas Buckthorn and Krystee kissing."

"Oh. Is that all?"

"Is that all! She's my best friend, he's supposed to be my boyfriend, and Dad is in Afghanistan, and that's so far away, and he hardly talked to me last night because it was all about you, and I miss him, and I'm just *miserable.*" The last word comes out on a sob, and Dakota buries her face against her knees again.

Sprig is speechless. She has never heard such an outburst from Dakota, but what really hits her is that Dakota misses Dad too. "You miss Dad," Sprig blurts. "You really do miss him."

"Duuh," Dakota cries, lifting her head. "What do you think! I miss him something awful."

"But I thought — I mean, you never say anything about Dad being away, and you never cry."

"Of course I don't," Dakota says fiercely. "I'm the older sister, I can't do that! Mom depends on me. I have to set an example."

"But —" Sprig starts, then closes her mouth. She doesn't know what to say. So many things

are happening in ways she doesn't expect —
like the kisses, and how different Russell acted,
and the way she made up with Bliss, and now
her sister. It's almost as if Sprig didn't even
know Dakota, didn't know anything about her.
Dakota isn't a hard-hearted stinker. Not. At. All.
She cares. She really cares.

Sprig scooches under the table and puts her
arms around her sister, and Dakota lets
her. She leans against Sprig and sighs. After a
moment, she says, "How long has Dad been
away now?"

"Three weeks and two days," Sprig says.
"And five hours," she adds.

"I knew you'd know." Dakota sniffles up a
few tears and swipes the back of her hand
under her nose. "Do you have a tissue? I'm a
mess." She is too, tears and snot are all over
her face.

Sprig checks her pockets. Empty, not even a
single chocolate kiss left. She could get up and
find a napkin, but she just doesn't feel like leaving Dakota. She pulls off her socks and hands
them to her sister. "Just use the top part," she

advises. "One for the eyes and one for the nose."

"I can't blow my nose on your cute socks," Dakota says.

"Yes, you can," Sprig says. "It's either that, or your new glitter shirt."

23

THE SAME
SKY

AFTER Sprig and Dakota decide to leave the party early, Dakota calls Mom on her cell, and they go outside to wait for her. "Are your feet cold without your socks?" Dakota asks.

"Not much," Sprig says. The socks are balled up in her jacket pocket. She looks up at the sky. Clouds are passing over the moon. "Do you think Dad is seeing the same sky we are?"

"I hope so," Dakota says.

They're silent for a few minutes, then Sprig says, "You know what, Dakota. I forgot to tell you something. I don't think it was Krystee's fault about kissing Buckthorn."

"Oh, please!"

"No, listen, Dakota. He was kissing everyone, any girl he could get. Krystee was just one of many." Wow, she's defending the Bad Influence! It's the right thing to do, though. She's sure Dad would approve. "Buckthorn was trying to set a record, Dakota, like it was for the Olympics."

"A *record*?"

"He probably just grabbed Krystee before she even knew what was happening. He wanted to kiss me too."

"You? I don't believe it. You just made that up to make me feel better about Krystee."

"Dakota, I didn't. On my honor. I was going to be number seven."

"Euuuw, I hate him! But he's so cute," she sighs.

"Lots of boys are cute," Sprig says. "Buckthorn is a kissing machine."

Her sister takes her arm. "So are you saying I ought to forgive Krystee?"

"Yes, if she's your true, best friend, then you should make up with her. But, first, you should talk to her. Don't just keep your feelings to yourself. Other people can't always tell what you're feeling, especially if you don't talk to them. Oh, and it helps if you have something to share, like chocolate kisses."

"Wow, you really are smart." Dakota squeezes Sprig's hand. "In case I forgot to tell you, you're really a great sister."

24

BLUE
MOUSE

MOM orders in Chinese take-out from Su Lin's on Friday night for the dinner party. Sprig and Dakota empty all the paper cartons into serving bowls. "Much prettier," Mom says, arranging the bowls on the dining room table. The two girls set out plates and silver and glasses, and put music on the stereo, and by the time the guests arrive, Sprig and Mom are ready to greet them at the door. They're all going to eat and then look at the DVD Dad sent home about his first two weeks in Afghanistan.

Mr. and Mrs. Hampler, Krystee's parents, are much smaller than Sprig expected. And nicer too. Can Krystee really be their daughter? "Dakota's still combing her hair," Sprig tells her, and Krystee bounds up the stairs. Bliss's mother kisses Sprig, and her father ruffles Sprig's hair and calls her "Buddy," as in, "How ya doin', Buddy?"

"Daaad," Bliss says, but Sprig just laughs. She likes bearded Mr. Gardner.

Dakota and Krystee go over to help Miss Ruthie, who's just home from the hospital. Her niece Roberta will be coming to stay with her, but meanwhile, she needs help going up and down stairs. As soon as Miss Ruthie comes in, she holds out her arms to hug Sprig. "My little hero," she says, and she starts telling the Hamplers and Gardners the whole story of that Saturday when she had a stroke. "And guess who saved my life!"

"This is so embarrassing," Sprig whispers to Bliss.

"Oh, come on, you love it," Bliss says.

"Everyone, sit wherever you want to," Mom says. "We're not formal here. Girls, if you don't want to stay at the table, that's fine." Krystee and Dakota immediately take their food and leave, but Bliss and Sprig decide to stay. What a mistake! The grown-ups can't stop talking about how good Miss Ruthie looks, and what they've read about Afghanistan, and how marvelous it is that Dad is keeping a documentary record for the family.

"Let's leave," Sprig whispers to Bliss, and they retreat upstairs to the bedroom. "That was so boring," Sprig says.

"Tell me about it!" They sit on the floor, backs against the bed, plates on their outstretched legs. "Now we can really talk," Bliss says.

"So what do you think?" Sprig asks, picking up a thread of a previous conversation. "Is Russell just a friend, or is he something else?"

"Friend to me," Bliss says. "Good friend, but you'll always be my best friend."

"Same here," Sprig says. "But you know, those kisses —"

"I think they were friendly kisses."

"Me too. I hope so, anyway, because, well, like my mom says, we've got plenty of time for boys —"

"Boys?" Dakota says, walking in with Krystee. She goes over to her bureau and opens the top drawer. "Are you talking about boys?" She takes out a scarf and wraps it around her hair.

"Never mind what we're talking about," Sprig says.

"Yeah, it's boys," Krystee says. "Look at their faces, they're all red! Come on, you two, tell! What boy is it? What's his name? Huh? Huh?"

"Oh, let's leave them alone," Dakota says, and the older girls leave.

"You know what," Bliss says. "We should have a code for talking about you-know-who, so other people don't get in on our private conversations. We could call him —" Bliss thinks for a moment "— the giraffe, and every time we want to talk about him, we'll say, 'the giraffe' —"

"Russell, a giraffe?" Sprig says. "We might as well call him a blue mouse."

"Perfect," Bliss says. "Do you think blue mouse has been different since the party?"

"Different how?"

"Well, blue mouse was so nice that night —"

"Did I hear you say *blue mouse*?" Dakota says, sticking her head in the door.

"You've been eavesdropping!" Sprig cries.

"Now, now," Dakota says, glancing over her shoulder at Krystee. "Would I do that?"

"Just tell us who blue mouse is," Krystee coaxes.

Sprig and Bliss look at each other and shrug. "Us to know, you to wonder," Bliss says.

"If you don't tell us, you can just leave this room," Dakota says.

"I'm so sorry," Sprig says, so sweetly she makes her teeth ache, "but it's your turn to sleep in the study. On the floor," she adds.

"Don't you want to switch with us?" Dakota says. "You had so much fun last time."

"Now *you* can have the fun," Sprig says.

"Brats," Dakota says. "Let's go, Krystee."

"Shut the door behind you," Sprig calls.

"Nice going," Bliss says.

"Thank you," Sprig says. "Now where were we? Oh, yes, we were talking about blue mouse. . . ."

This book was designed by Leyah Jensen.

The text was set in Lomba Book.
The display font was set in

Pink Flamingo
and
FINK SANS.